MR. LEMONCELLO'S LIBRARY OLYMPICS

OTHER BOOKS BY CHRIS GRABENSTEIN

Escape from Mr. Lemoncello's Library
The Island of Dr. Libris

THE HAUNTED MYSTERY SERIES
The Crossroads
The Hanging Hill
The Smoky Corridor
The Black Heart Crypt

CO-AUTHORED WITH JAMES PATTERSON
Daniel X: Armageddon
Daniel X: Lights Out
I Funny
I Even Funnier
I Totally Funniest
I Funny TV
Treasure Hunters
Treasure Hunters: Danger Down the Nile
Treasure Hunters: Secrets of the Forbidden City
House of Robots
House of Robots: Robots Go Wild!

MR. LEMONCELLO'S LIBRARY OLYMPICS

CHRIS GRABENSTEIN

RANDOM HOUSE NEW YORK

Text copyright © 2016 by Chris Grabenstein
Jacket art copyright © 2016 by Gilbert Ford
Photograph credit: p. 269 (MAD #105) ™ and © E. C. Publications, Inc.

Visit us on the Web! randomhousekids.com

Educators and librarians, for a variety of teaching tools, visit us at RHTeachersLibrarians.com

Library of Congress Cataloging-in-Publication Data
Grabenstein, Chris.
Mr. Lemoncello's Library Olympics / Chris Grabenstein. — First edition.
p. cm
Summary: "Mr. Lemoncello has invited teams from all across America to compete in the first-ever Library Olympics . . . but someone is trying to censor what the kids are reading."— Provided by publisher
ISBN 978-0-553-51040-9 (trade) — ISBN 978-0-553-51041-6 (lib. bdg.) — ISBN 978-0-553-51043-0 (ebook) — ISBN 978-0-399-55650-0 (intl. tr. pbk.)
[1. Libraries—Fiction. 2. Contests—Fiction. 3. Books and reading—Fiction. 4. Censorship—Fiction. 5. Eccentrics and eccentricities—Fiction.] I. Title.
PZ7.G7487Mr 2016 [Fic]—dc23 2015024473

Printed in the United States of America
10 9 8 7 6 5 4 3 2 1
First Edition

For Sunshine Cavalluzzi, Sid Reischer, Stacey Rattner,
and all the awesome parents, teachers, and librarians
who do so much to make reading fun

And in memory of Rosanne Macrina,
the longtime librarian at P.S. 10 in Brooklyn,
who inspired so many children and one author
who was very lucky to have met her

MR. LEMONCELLO'S
LIBRARY
OLYMPICS

Just about every kid in America wished they could be Kyle Keeley.

Especially when he zoomed across their TV screens as a flaming squirrel in a holiday commercial for Squirrel Squad Six, the hysterically crazy new Lemoncello video game.

Kyle's friends Akimi Hughes and Sierra Russell were also in that commercial. They thumbed controllers and tried to blast Kyle out of the sky. He dodged every rubber band, coconut custard pie, mud clod, and wadded-up sock ball they flung his way.

It was awesome.

In the commercial for Mr. Lemoncello's See Ya, Wouldn't Want to Be Ya board game, Kyle starred as the yellow pawn. His head became the bubble tip at the top of the playing piece. Kyle's buddy Miguel Fernandez was

1

the green pawn. Kyle and Miguel slid around the life-size game like hockey pucks. When Miguel landed on the same square as Kyle, that meant Kyle's pawn had to be bumped back to the starting line.

"See ya!" shouted Miguel. "Wouldn't want to be ya!"

Kyle was yanked up off the ground by a hidden cable and hurled backward, soaring above the board.

It was also awesome.

But Kyle's absolute favorite starring role was in the commercial for Mr. Lemoncello's You Seriously Can't Say That game, where the object was to get your teammates to guess the word on your card without using any of the forbidden words listed on the same card.

Akimi, Sierra, Miguel, and the perpetually perky Haley Daley sat on a circular couch and played the guessers. Kyle stood in front of them as the clue giver.

"Salsa," said Kyle.

"Nachos!" said Akimi.

A buzzer sounded. Akimi's guess was wrong.

Kyle tried again. "Horseradish sauce!"

"Something nobody ever eats," said Haley.

Another buzzer.

Kyle goofed up and said one of the forbidden words: "Ketchup!"

SPLAT! Fifty gallons of syrupy, goopy tomato sauce slimed him from above. It oozed down his face and dribbled off his ears.

Everybody laughed. So Kyle, who loved being the class

clown almost as much as he loved playing (and winning) Mr. Lemoncello's wacky games, went ahead and read the whole list of banned words as quickly as he could.

"Mustard-mayonnaise-pickle-relish."

SQUOOSH! He was drenched by buckets of yellow glop, white sludge, and chunky green gunk. The slop slid along his sleeves, trickled into his pants, and puddled on the floor.

His four friends busted a gut laughing at Kyle, who was soaked in more "condiments" (the word on his card) than a mile-long hot dog.

"Was it fun?" boomed an off-camera announcer.

"Fun?" answered Haley. "Hello? It's a Lemoncello!"

That's how all the commercials ended, with Haley saying the slogan "Hello? It's a Lemoncello!" She became a TV superstar. People all across America wished they could be Haley Daley, too. Except, of course, for the kids who were extremely jealous of her and wondered why she, Kyle Keeley, Akimi Hughes, Sierra Russell, and Miguel Fernandez had been chosen to star in Mr. Lemoncello's holiday commercials.

When they found out that becoming famous TV stars was the prize the five kids had won in a game played at Mr. Lemoncello's incredible new library in Alexandria-ville, Ohio—a game they hadn't been invited to play—they started demanding a rematch.

2

Charles Chiltington sat in his family's home theater watching his classmate Kyle Keeley rocket across a seventy-inch plasma-screen TV.

It was the worst Christmas vacation of his life.

For over a month, whenever he clicked on the television, Charles was forced to look at the five cheaters who, six months earlier, had robbed him of his rightful prize.

In that night's Lemoncello commercial, Keeley—the ringleader of the group that had "defeated" Charles in the Escape from Mr. Lemoncello's Library game—looked ridiculous dressed up in goofy goggles like a flying squirrel. But Keeley was obviously having a grand time starring in the commercial.

A commercial *Charles* should've starred in.

Keeley had needed four teammates to best Charles in

the past June's escape game, which was played inside the silly game maker's even sillier new library on its opening weekend.

Keeley had also needed Mr. Lemoncello's help to win.

At the very last second, just as Charles was nearing victory, the batty billionaire disqualified him on a trumped-up technicality. Keeley and his cronies went on to win the game and the grand prize.

Charles, on the other hand, went home to hear what a disappointment he was to his father.

Because Chiltingtons never lose.

Especially not to ordinary nobodies like Kyle Keeley.

For six months, Charles had been plotting his revenge on Keeley and his teammates: smart-aleck Akimi Hughes, library geek Miguel Fernandez, bookworm Sierra Russell, and most especially turncoat traitor Haley Daley, who had been on Charles's team with Andrew Peckleman until she deserted them to join Team Kyle.

"Mr. Lemoncello robbed me," Charles muttered miserably. "They should shut down his ludicrous library."

He'd been miserably muttering the same thing ever since the Lemoncello holiday commercials started airing. But for some reason, watching this annoying squirrel commercial made a new thought bubble up inside his brain.

He pushed the pause button on the DVR remote.

They should shut down Mr. Lemoncello.

That was a better idea.

The good citizens of Alexandriaville, Ohio, should not allow the demented Mr. Lemoncello to continue to control what went on inside their new *public* library.

Yes! His mind started whirring. That was the perfect angle. A public campaign to wrench control of the library away from the dangerous lunatic Luigi Lemoncello.

And Charles knew just who should lead the charge.

His mother.

She had a long history of championing public causes.

When he was in kindergarten, she had led the Anti-Cupcake Crusade, because Charles liked brownies better. When he was in third grade, his mother had made certain that the teacher who dared give Charles a B on his papier-mâché volcano was fired. And in fourth grade, she had yanked him out of Chumley Prep (and cut off their endowment) when the private school had the nerve to hire a history teacher who celebrated International Talk Like a Pirate Day.

Plus, Charles's mother did not particularly care for what Mr. Lemoncello was doing inside his zany library.

"Too much sizzle, not enough steak," she'd complained to friends in her bridge club. "They also lend out too many of the wrong sort of books."

Wheels were spinning inside Charles's head as he plotted his next moves.

With just the slightest nudge, taking the "Lemoncello" out of the Lemoncello Library would become his mother's next great cause. He was certain of it.

"Mummy?" he called out in his best your-little-boy-has-a-boo-boo voice.

When no one answered, he did it again. Louder.

"Mummy! Make it go away! I'm being traumatized! Mummy!"

His mother bustled into the TV room. "Charles, darling? What's the matter?"

Charles pointed a trembling finger at the TV screen. "Mr. Lemoncello. Make him go away. His library is a petrifying place full of cheaters!"

"I know, dear, but there's nothing . . ."

Charles started blubbering. "He cheated me, Mummy. He robbed me!"

"Yes, honey . . ."

It was time to pull out the heavy artillery.

"He lowered my self-esteem! I feel like such a failure!" He sniffled. "Because of Mr. Lemoncello, I may never go to college!"

His mother's face turned ghostly white. *Score!*

"Hush now. Mummy's here. Everything will be all right."

She hugged him tightly.

Charles grinned.

Mr. Lemoncello was toast.

Burnt toast with toe-jam jelly on top.

3

With school out for the winter holidays, Kyle and his friends were spending a lot of time hanging out downtown at the Lemoncello Library, where, because of their celebrity status, every day was a cake day.

Cake days were a Keeley family tradition. Whenever one of them did something spectacular—like his brother Mike winning a football game (again) or his other brother, Curtis, getting straight A's (again)—Kyle's mom baked a cake.

Ever since Kyle and his teammates had won the escape game, every day had felt that way. Cakey.

"You're the dude from the commercial!" at least a dozen kids said to Kyle as he strolled through the Rotunda Reading Room.

He gave them each a jaunty two-finger salute. He'd seen movie stars do the same kind of salute on TV.

"Can I have your autograph?" said a little girl.

"Sure. Here you go."

Kyle still signed each and every autograph individually.

His best friend, Akimi, on the other hand, passed out preprinted signature cards. "It's faster that way," she said.

"Hi, Kyle!" Sierra was curled up in one of the cozy chairs near the three-story-tall wall of fiction. She was reading a book, of course. Her gaze was far-off and dreamy, because when Sierra Russell was into a book, she was totally *into* it. She practically crawled between the covers to live with the characters.

"Hey," said Kyle. "What're you reading?"

"Actually, I'm *re*reading *Bud, Not Buddy* by Christopher Paul Curtis. It's my favorite."

"Sweet."

"Have you ever read it?"

"Not yet. But it's on my list."

Sierra laughed. Probably because Kyle Keeley had the longest to-be-read list of any kid in the country.

"There's another copy on the shelf," said Sierra.

"That's okay. I'm meeting Akimi and Miguel upstairs in the Electronic Learning Center. Mr. Lemoncello just installed a new educational video game: Charlemagne's Chivalry. I think it's about the Knights of the Round Table."

"Um, Kyle? Charlemagne was the Holy Roman Emperor. *King Arthur* had the round table—in *England*."

"See? You *can* learn something new every day. Catch

9

you later, Sierra. Don't want to keep Charlemagne or King Arthur waiting."

Kyle bounded up the spiral staircase to the third floor, signing autographs and posing for selfies with fans along the way.

He passed through the two very thick sliding glass doors that stopped the wild sounds of the Electronic Learning Center from leaking out into the rest of the building.

Once he was inside the arcade, Kyle's ears were bombarded by the blare, buzz, and bells of three dozen educational video games. His nose was blasted, too. A lot of the games in the ELC were equipped with Mr. Lemoncello's newest sensation, smell-a-vision, including one where you were a royal rat with body-odor issues, swimming through English history via the sewers of London.

"I'm sorry, I can't sign another autograph or my hand will fall off," said Haley Daley, who was holding court near the Cleopatra: Queen of the Nile game console.

Kyle didn't play that one too much, because Haley Daley always outscored him. She knew the trick for summoning crocodiles up from the Nile.

"Kyle?" Haley waved at him. "You got a second?"

"I'm supposed to meet—"

"This is super important."

Kyle made his way to Haley.

"I'm moving!" she said.

"Seriously?"

"Hello? Do you know how many offers I've had since I starred in those commercials for Mr. Lemoncello?"

"Actually, we all kind of starred in—"

"Hundreds. Maybe thousands. So my whole family's going to Hollywood. My dad found a new job in L.A. Plus, my agent is already booking guest spots for me on the Disney Channel."

"Awesome," said Kyle.

Haley Daley and her family had needed the money that came with winning the library escape game more than any other player had. It sounded like Mr. Lemoncello's generosity had really turned things around for them.

"I just wanted to say goodbye. And thanks, Kyle."

"Hey, it was a team effort. We won it together."

"Whatever. I gotta go. Need to pick out a new pair of sunglasses."

Haley dramatically waved goodbye to Kyle and all her adoring fans as she traipsed out of the Electronic Learning Center. She did that dramatically, too.

"Yo, Kyle? We need a little help over here, bro! Like now."

Miguel and Akimi were on the far side of the Electronic Learning Center playing Charlemagne's Chivalry. Miguel had the stubby controller rod gripped in front of his chest, wielding it like a lightsaber.

Kyle hustled across the noisy room.

"What's up?"

"Charlemagne needs a champion," explained Akimi. "Someone who will defend the weak and defenseless, fight for what's right, yadda yadda. The game is based on the ancient code of chivalry."

"I'm kind of stuck," said Miguel, fending off a fiery dragon with his virtual sword swishes.

"And I'm kind of bored," said Akimi. "See you two later."

Kyle turned to Miguel. "What are your options?"

"Slay the dragon or go feed the hungry peasants."

"No contest. Slay the dragon."

"You sure?"

"Definitely. If you don't, the dragon will kill the peasants. You slay the dragon, the peasants will rejoice. Peasants always love dragon slayers."

"Okay. If you say so."

Miguel thrust his imaginary sword forward. His on-screen knight pierced the dragon's hide with his steel blade.

The animated dragon fizzled out a geyser of gas and shriveled into a heap of crinkled plastic.

"Aw, man. It wasn't a real dragon. It was a big balloon. Like in the Macy's parade . . ."

A swarm of peasants armed with pitchforks stormed across the screen. They attacked Miguel's knight.

"Why didst thou not bringeth us food?" screamed the leader of the peasant army. "Death to the selfish, unchivalrous knave!"

Kyle heard the unmistakable *BLOOP-BLOOP-BLOOP*

sound of video-game death. Miguel's knight took a pitchfork in the butt and wilted into a heap of pixels.

"Okay," said Kyle. "Now that we know what *not* to do, we'll play again and win."

"Why bother? We don't need Charlemagne to tell us we're champions. Am I right?"

Kyle grinned. "Totally."

Then the two of them knocked knuckles and chanted the lyrics to their favorite classic-rock tune: "*We are the champions, my friend. . . .*"

On the Monday after New Year's, Kyle stood shivering at his bus stop.

Ohio gets very cold and slushy in January.

Finally, the bus pulled up and swung open its door.

"Well, hel-lo," said Mrs. Logan, the driver. "It's another Lemon-cel-lo!"

Kyle shook his head. Bus drivers watched TV commercials, too.

"Good morning, Mrs. Logan," said Kyle, climbing up the steps.

"Got a riddle for you." Ever since his team had won the Lemoncello Library game, *everybody* was constantly trying to trip them up with riddles and puzzles.

"Go for it," said Kyle.

"What two things can you never eat for breakfast?"

"Easy," said Kyle. "Lunch and dinner."

Mrs. Logan waved her arm at him. "Ah, go sit down."

Kyle high-fived his way up the bus aisle to his usual seat, next to Akimi. Sierra sat behind Akimi, her nose buried in another book.

"What are you reading?" Kyle asked. "That *Butter Not Nutty Buddy* book?"

"Actually," said Sierra, "I'm *re*reading *Charlie and the Chocolate Factory,* because everybody keeps saying Mr. Lemoncello reminds them of Willy Wonka. But Mr. Lemoncello is much kinder."

"And he doesn't have Oompa-Loompas," quipped Akimi.

"Or Augustus Gloop," added Kyle.

"Actually," said Akimi, "I think Charles Chiltington was our Augustus."

"Really?" said Sierra. "He reminds me more of Veruca Salt."

Wow. Sierra Russell cracked a joke. She had definitely loosened up since joining Team Kyle.

"So," said Akimi after Kyle peeled off his parka, "did your grandmother give you that sweater for Christmas?"

"How'd you guess?"

"It looks like something you'd buy at a pet store. For a dog named Fluffy."

"I think I might lose it in my locker today."

"Good idea."

"Um, excuse me?" said Alexa Mehlman, a sixth grader seated across the aisle from Kyle.

15

"Hey, Alexa," said Kyle. "What's up?"

"I don't mean to bother you. . . ."

"It's no bother. What can I do for you?"

"Well, my uncle gave me Mr. Lemoncello's Phenomenal Picture Word Puzzler for Chanukah and I can't figure out this one rebus."

"Let me see it."

"The category is 'famous slogans,'" said Alexa, passing a cardboard square to Kyle. It was filled with a jumble of letters and pictograms.

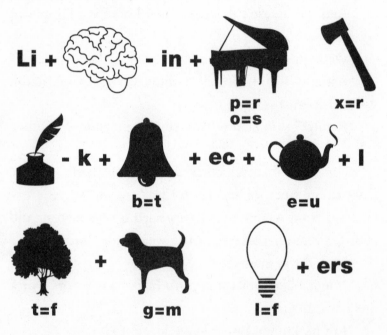

"The first word is 'librarians,'" said Akimi. "L-I plus B-R-A-I-N minus I-N gives you L-I-B-R-A. Then you add P-I-A-N-O, but make the 'P' an 'R' and the 'O' an 'S,'

"Um, because they don't live here in Alexandriaville?" said Akimi.

"Only seventh graders at this school were eligible to enter the essay contest to win a spot at the library lock-in," added Sierra.

For the first twelve years of the Alexandriaville seventh graders' lives, school media centers were the only libraries they had ever known. The old public library, the one Mr. Lemoncello had loved when he was a boy growing up in the small Ohio town, had been bulldozed to make way for a multilevel concrete parking structure.

"They just wish they could be us," said Kyle. "You can't really blame 'em."

"It's worse," said Miguel. "They think they could've *beaten* us."

Miguel waved for his friends to follow him to the rows of computer terminals.

"I was Googling us again this morning, and all these blogs and posts started popping up. None of them are very nice."

"Greetings, heroes!" called Mrs. Yunghans, the middle school librarian, who absolutely *loved* having the most famous library card holders in America checking out books in her library. "Don't believe all those nasty things people are writing about you kids on the Web. They're just jealous."

Kyle and his teammates huddled around a monitor while Miguel clacked the keyboard.

19

"Check it out."

They scrolled through the top search results for "Escape from Mr. Lemoncello's Library."

"It took them a whole day to find their way out of the library?" wrote one blogger.

"I could've done it in half a day," commented another.

"I demand a rematch," said more.

"This isn't fair, Mr. Lemoncello."

"We demand a chance!"

"Put *us* in that library. We could beat Team Kyle with one 612.97 tied behind our back."

"That's the closest Dewey decimal number for hand," explained Miguel. "Actually, it refers to regional physiology of the upper extremities."

"Wow," said Kyle. "What a bunch of library nerds."

Miguel cleared his throat, prompting Kyle to quickly add, "Not that there's anything wrong with that."

"Ouch," said Akimi. "Listen to this one."

She clicked open a post with even the subject line screaming in all caps.

" 'KEELEY'S TEAM ONLY WON BECAUSE THEY CHEATED!' " she read aloud. " 'MR. LEMONCELLO IS BLATANTLY LYING TO THE WORLD ABOUT WHAT REALLY HAPPENED ON THAT DREADFUL, GHASTLY, AND ABOMINABLE DAY LAST SUMMER. HE SHOULD BE TARRED AND FEATHERED AND RUN OUT OF TOWN ON A RAIL.' "

"That's horrible," said Sierra.

"Of course it is," said Akimi. "Look who wrote it."
She pointed to the semi-anonymous signature: "C.C."
Charles Chiltington.

6

Dr. Yanina Zinchenko, the world-famous librarian, dragged a lumpy mail sack to the far end of the Rotunda Reading Room, where her boss, Luigi Lemoncello, was flying up and down in front of the three-story-tall fiction bookcases.

"I'm looking for a good book," said Mr. Lemoncello as his hover ladder jerked vertically, then skittered sideways. "But I'm not exactly sure what I'm looking for."

The hover ladders were floating platforms with handrails, book baskets, and ski-boot safety locks that allowed you to float up to retrieve any book you wanted simply by entering the book's call number into a computerized keypad. The system worked with the same magnetic levitation technology used in Germany and Japan to propel bullet trains with magnets instead of wheels.

"Perhaps I can be of assistance," said Dr. Zinchenko in her thick Russian accent. "Do you have the call number?"

"No need," Mr. Lemoncello said, laughing. "I wanted to test-drive our new 'browse' function."

After several patrons had complained that the hover ladders' demand for a specific book code eliminated the ability for patrons to leisurely peruse the shelves, the imagineers at Mr. Lemoncello's game company had come up with the new and improved hover ladders, which featured a browse button.

Once you pushed it, the hover ladder randomly flitted in front of the shelves, using advanced biofeedback technology, heart-rate monitors, and complex algorithms to figure out what sort of story you might be interested in.

"But we have a very important matter to discuss." Dr. Zinchenko pointed to the mail sack. It was the size of an overstuffed duffel bag.

"Oh, dear. A V.I.M.? I don't know if I have the vigor for a V.I.M."

"We also have visitors. . . ."

"Visitors and a V.I.M.? I'll deal with both as soon as I finish browsing."

"Mr. Lemoncello?" bellowed a voice below.

He glanced down and saw a very properly dressed lady flanked by six other very properly dressed ladies and one properly dressed man in a bow tie.

"I'll be right with you!" shouted Mr. Lemoncello as his

hover ladder caromed across the wall of books like an out-of-control Ping-Pong ball. "I'm busy browsing."

"My name is Susana Chiltington," the lady said operatically. "Mrs. Susana *Willoughby* Chiltington."

"Hello, Susana. Don't you cry for me. The doctors say they can easily remove the banjo on my knee."

Mrs. Chiltington wasn't amused.

"Perhaps you've heard of my brother?" she said. "The head librarian for the Library of Congress? James F. Willoughby the third?"

"What happened to the first two?"

"I beg your pardon?"

"Never mind. I am finished browsing. Pull me down, Captain Underpants."

The hover ladder gently lowered the happy billionaire to the floor.

"Now then, how may I help you, Duchess Susana Willoughby Chiltington the third, Esquire, PhD?"

"I'm not a . . . Oh, never mind. My colleagues and I represent the recently formed League of Concerned Library Lovers. Winthrop?"

The gentleman in the bow tie opened a leather briefcase. "As a public library, Mr. Lemoncello, this institution needs a board of trustees to oversee its finances and champion its mission."

Mrs. Chiltington snorted a little. "It is quite customary."

"So is pumpkin pie on Thanksgiving, but I prefer pineapple rhubarb," said Mr. Lemoncello.

"As concerned library lovers," said the gentleman, brandishing a thick document, "we are here today to volunteer our services."

Mr. Lemoncello ignored the man and focused on Mrs. Chiltington.

"You're Charles's mother, aren't you?"

"Indeed." She snuffled and adjusted her clothes to make certain all the seams were lined up precisely the way they were supposed to be.

"Might I humbly suggest, Mrs. Chiltington, that your considerable concern might be better spent on your son instead of my library? Now then, Dr. Zinchenko, I believe we have a very important matter to discuss?"

"Yes, sir."

Mr. Lemoncello walked over to the wall of bookshelves and tilted back the head on a marble bust of Andrew Carnegie, revealing a red button hidden in his neck.

"Mr. Lemoncello?" trilled Mrs. Chiltington. "A public library requires public oversight—guardians who will safeguard the institution's well-being and stability."

"I know! I've been thinking about that very fact for months. I've also been thinking about lunch for at least fifteen minutes. I thank you for your time and concern."

He bopped the red button.

A door-sized segment of bookshelves swished sideways. Mr. Lemoncello and Dr. Zinchenko disappeared with the mailbag down a dimly lit corridor. The bookcase slammed shut behind them.

"Mr. Lemoncello?" Mrs. Chiltington called after them. "Dr. Zinchenko?"

She banged on a row of books as if she were knocking on a door.

"Mr. Lemoncello!"

A burly security guard—maybe six four, 250 pounds, his hair in long, ropy dreadlocks—came up behind her.

"Ma'am? I'm going to have to ask you to leave the library if you keep punching the books."

Mrs. Chiltington swung around.

"I'm not . . . Oh, never mind."

She glanced at the guard's name tag.

"Clarence?"

"Yes, ma'am."

"Well, Clarence, don't worry. We're leaving. But kindly inform Mr. Lemoncello that we shall return."

"Wonderful," said Clarence. "Mr. Lemoncello loves it when people come back to visit his library."

Mrs. Chiltington gave Clarence a frosty smile.

"I'm sure he does. And next time, there will be more of us!"

7

Early in the second week of January, each member of Team Kyle received a thick envelope in the mail.

When they opened it, they found an engraved invitation:

SPLENDIFEROUS GREETINGS AND SALUTATIONS!

YOU AND YOUR FAMILY ARE HEREBY
CHERRY CORDIALLY INVITED TO THE
ANNOUNCEMENT OF MY STUPENDOUS NEW NEWS.

FRIDAY NIGHT
SHALL WE SAY 7-ISH?

THE ROTUNDA READING ROOM OF
THE LEMONCELLO LIBRARY

REFRESHMENTS SHALL BE SERVED,
INCLUDING CHERRY CORDIALS.

AND THERE *WILL* BE BALLOONS.

———————

REGARDS,
LUIGI L. LEMONCELLO

* * *

Friday evening, Kyle and his family piled into their minivan and drove downtown to the library.

"Isn't this exciting?" said Kyle's mother. "I should've baked a cake."

"Any idea what the big announcement is?" asked his dad.

"Not a clue," said Kyle. "But we're hoping Mr. Lemoncello is going to ask us to star in more TV commercials."

"Please, no," moaned Kyle's brother Mike. "Your head's big enough already."

Snowflakes swirled in the misty beams of light flooding the front of the domed building that used to be a bank until Mr. Lemoncello turned it into a library. Kyle noticed several TV news satellite trucks taking up the parking spaces along the curb.

"You better get in there, Kyle," said his dad. "We'll go find a place to park."

"Have fun!" added his mom.

Kyle dashed up the marble steps and into the library's lobby.

Miguel and Sierra were waiting for him near the life-size statue of Mr. Lemoncello perched atop a lily pad in a reflecting pool. The statue's head was tilted back so the bronze Mr. Lemoncello could squirt an arc of water out of his mouth like he was a human drinking fountain. His motto was chiseled into the statue's pedestal:

KNOWLEDGE NOT SHARED REMAINS UNKNOWN.
—LUIGI L. LEMONCELLO

"Hey, Kyle!" exclaimed Miguel. "The place is packed. Everybody was invited! All twelve of the original players."

"Including Charles Chiltington?" asked Kyle.

"He's a no-show."

"I hope Andrew Peckleman doesn't show up, either," said Sierra with a slight shiver. Peckleman had been Chiltington's ally in the escape game and had tricked Sierra out of her library card so he could spy on Team Kyle.

"He was definitely invited," said Miguel. "But he won't be coming. Ever since he got kicked out of the game, Andrew doesn't really like libraries. He even quit being a library aide at school."

"That's sad," said Sierra.

"You guys," said Akimi, coming in from the Rotunda Reading Room, "there's all sorts of TV news crews inside. Including that reporter from CNN."

"Which one?"

"The guy with the hair."

"And there's food in the Book Nook Café," said Miguel. "Tons of it."

"So why are we hanging out here?" said Kyle. "Let's go."

The four friends hurried under the arch that led into the vast Rotunda Reading Room. The rotunda was packed. Clusters of brightly colored balloons were tethered to the green-shaded lamps on the reading desks. Hidden surround-sound speakers blasted a brassy, heroic fanfare.

Overhead, the Wonder Dome was a fluttering display of fifty state flags flapping against a cloudless blue sky, where, for whatever reason, a very muscular couple in ancient robes rode a chariot back and forth across the curved ceiling like it was a horse-drawn comet. They reminded Kyle of a Greek god and goddess straight out of the Percy Jackson books.

"Wow," said Miguel. "Do you think Rick Riordan's going to be here? That would be so awesome!"

All the animated action was displayed on ten wedge-shaped high-definition video screens—as luminous as any sports arena's scoreboard. They lined the underbelly of the building's colossal cathedral ceiling like glowing slices of pie. Each screen could showcase individual images or join with the other nine to create one spectacular presentation.

"Whoa," said Akimi. "Check out the statues. They're hardly wearing any clothes."

"And," Sierra said, "they look like they're made out of marble."

"Right," said Akimi. "*See-through* marble."

Tucked beneath the ten Wonder Dome screens in arched niches were ten 3-D statues glowing a ghostly green. Holograms.

"They all remind me of Hercules," said Kyle, taking in the dizzying array of muscular wrestlers, javelin throwers, discus flingers, and runners. "Except for the lady with the horse."

"I think that's a Spartan princess named Cynisca," said Sierra, who read a ton of history books, too. "She won the four-horse chariot race in 396 BC and again in 392 BC in what we call the ancient Olympic Games."

Akimi arched an eyebrow. "You sure she isn't that girl from *The Girl Who Loved Wild Horses*?"

Sierra laughed. "Positive!"

"Splendiferous greetings and salutations to one and all!" boomed Mr. Lemoncello's voice from the loudspeakers as the trumpets blared their final fanfare. "Thank you for joining us this evening. It is now time for my big, colossal, and jumbo-sized announcement!"

Kyle held his breath and crossed his fingers.

He really hoped he and his friends were going to star in more commercials.

Being famous was fun.

And kind of easy, too.

8

Blazing circles of bright light swung across the second-floor balcony to shine on Mr. Lemoncello.

Spotlights following him, he scampered to the nearest spiral staircase, slid down the banister, and dismounted with an impressive backflip. When his boot heels hit the ground, they squawked like a chicken, then mooed like a cow.

"Dr. Zinchenko? Kindly remind me never to borrow boots from Old MacDonald again."

Mr. Lemoncello wore a bright red and blue Revolutionary War outfit with a ruffled collar and a cape. A plumed tricorne hat completed the costume. He pulled out a brass handbell and rang it. Loudly.

"Welcome, boys and girls, families and friends, esteemed members of the press."

Mr. Lemoncello smiled for all the television cameras aimed at him.

"Clarence? Clement?" He clanged his bell a few more times. "Please bring in today's mail."

Clarence and Clement, the beefy twins who headed up security for the Lemoncello Library, marched into the Rotunda Reading Room flanked by six robotic carts loaded down with United States Postal Service mail bins.

"Dr. Zinchenko? How many emails have we received on this same subject?"

Dr. Zinchenko consulted the very advanced smartphone clipped to the waistband of her bright red pantsuit. "Close to one million, sir."

"One million?" Mr. Lemoncello shuddered. "And that's just the bad beginning. But, not to worry, I have come up with the happy ending! You see, fellow library lovers, kids all across this wondermous country are eager to prove that *they* are bibliophilic champions, too. Therefore, oyez, oyez, and hear ye, hear ye."

Kyle covered his ears. Mr. Lemoncello was clanging his bell like crazy.

"Let the word go forth from Alexandriaville to all fifty states. I, Mr. Luigi L. Lemoncello, master game maker extraordinaire, am proud to announce a series of games that will rekindle the spirit and glory of the ancient Olympic Games held, once upon a time, in Olympia—the one in Greece, not the capital of Washington State. Therefore,

I hereby proclaim the commencement of the first-ever Library Olympics! A competition that will discover, once and for all, who are this sweet land of liberty's true library champions. Dr. Zinchenko?"

"Yes, Mr. Lemoncello?"

"Kindly invite your network of crackerjack librarians all across this country to organize regional competitions."

"Immediately, sir."

"Oh, it can wait until tomorrow. I, of course, will pay for everything, including the Cracker Jacks."

"Of course, sir."

"Bring me your best and brightest bookworms, research hounds, and gamers. Our first Library Olympiad shall commence on March twentieth. The ancient Greeks had their summer games, so we'll take the first day of spring."

"How many members should be on each team?" asked Dr. Zinchenko, who was furiously tapping notes into her tablet computer.

"Five," said Mr. Lemoncello, "the same number as on Team Kyle. Our hometown heroes are hereby officially invited to these Library Olympics, where they will defend their crown—which, to keep things Greek and chic, will be made out of olive branches."

Kyle gulped.

Another competition?

Against the top library nerds in the country?

He didn't like the sound of that. He liked being a champion and staying a champion.

"Um, sir?" said Miguel, raising his hand.

"Yes, Miguel?"

"Haley Daley moved to Hollywood. We're down to four."

"What about Andrew Peckleman?" asked Mr. Lemoncello. "He only cheated in the first game because someone who shall remain nameless bullied him into doing it."

Mr. Lemoncello pretended to cough, but his cough sounded a lot like *"Ch-arles Ch-iltington."*

"Andrew won't play," said Miguel. "He says he hates libraries."

"Oh, my. Well, we must certainly work on changing that. For now, we will stick with *four* members on every team. Just like the four horses pulling that Spartan lady Cynisca's chariot."

Yep, thought Kyle. *Sierra was right. Again.*

"Once we find our other Library Olympians," said Mr. Lemoncello, "we'll fly them here to Alexandriaville and commence our duodecimalthon."

"Your what?" asked Akimi.

"Duodecimalthon. It's like a decathlon, only with *twelve* games instead of ten."

"Why twelve?" asked Kyle, who was already trying to figure out how many games his team would need to win to keep its title.

"Because 'duodecimalthon' sounds a lot like 'Dewey decimal system' if you say it real fast with a mouthful of malted milk balls, don't you agree?"

"Yes, sir."

"Good," said Mr. Lemoncello, raising his bell and striking a heroic pose. "The four members of the winning team shall each receive a full scholarship to the college of their choice."

The audience applauded. Some parents even whistled.

"That's right. It's very whistle-worthy. The winners will receive four years of paid tuition plus free room, board, and books. Lots and lots of books. Now go find me my champions!"

9

Dr. Zinchenko went to work with her book- and game-loving librarian colleagues in all fifty states.

The country was divided up into seven regions: Midwest, Northeast, Mid-Atlantic, Southeast, Southwest, Mountain, and Pacific. Since the Library Olympics would be held to see if any team could dethrone the stars of Mr. Lemoncello's holiday commercials, only children in middle school, like the four members of Team Kyle, were allowed to participate.

Throughout January and February, thousands of eager contestants flocked to their local libraries to play the same kind of Dewey decimal scavenger-hunt game that had been at the heart of the Escape from Mr. Lemoncello's Library game.

In Decatur, Georgia, a girl named Diane Capriola advanced to the Southeast semifinals when she worked her way out of an Atlanta–Fulton County public library before anybody else by solving a riddle: "What occurs once in every minute, twice in every moment, yet never in a thousand years?"

"The answer, of course, is the letter 'M,' " Diane told local TV reporters. "So, I went to the reference section, opened up the 'M' encyclopedia, and—ta-da—there was a key to the back door tucked inside! When I stepped out to the sidewalk, the librarians were waiting with balloons and cake. It was easy-peasy."

In California, a boy named Pranav Pillai became a finalist for the Pacific team after he correctly deciphered that 683.3, the Dewey decimal code for *Louie the Locksmith's Big Book of Padlocks, Dead Bolts, and Tumblers,* was also the combination for the lock securing the exit of the Los Altos Public Library: 6-R, 8-L, 3-R, 3-L.

But the player librarians all over the country were raving about most was Marjory Muldauer from Bloomfield Hills, Michigan. A gangly seventh grader, a foot taller than any of her competitors, Marjory Muldauer had memorized the ten categories of the Dewey decimal system before she entered preschool.

The books in her bedroom were all organized by numbered codes. So were the spices in her mother's kitchen cabinets. And the baby food jars filled with nuts and bolts in her father's garage.

Marjory liked organizing things.

She knew her way around a library better than the robotic carts in Mr. Lemoncello's library. She read six books a day and could do two crossword puzzles at once—with a ballpoint pen.

"I'm glad that Mr. Lemoncello read my several letters and launched these Library Olympics," Marjory told a reporter from her hometown newspaper. "I could really use that college scholarship he's giving away. I'm also glad that the libraries where I've competed thus far have based their scavenger hunts on good old-fashioned research techniques. It's too bad that so many of the kids who signed up for the competition see these games as some kind of party."

"What do you mean?" asked the reporter.

"Mr. Lemoncello insists that everybody be given balloons and cake. Cake has no place in a library. Frosting is sticky. Sticky fingers damage books."

"But Mr. Lemoncello is also a great lover of libraries."

"Is he?" said Marjory skeptically. "I don't think Mr. Lemoncello loves libraries *qua* libraries."

"Huh?" said the reporter. "What does 'qua' mean?"

" 'As.' It's Latin. Mr. Lemoncello does not love libraries *as* libraries. He thinks they need to be tricked out with gadgets and gizmos and holographic displays. That library in Ohio reminds me of Disneyland with a few books. I think Mr. Lemoncello is seriously immature. He probably still believes in three-nine-eight-point-two."

"Huh?" The reporter was confused again.

"Three-nine-eight-point-two!" said Marjory. "It's the Dewey decimal number for fairy tales."

The reporter just nodded and closed her notepad.

Marjory Muldauer had that effect on people.

"Wait," Marjory told the reporter. "I'm not finished. Be sure you write this down: Kyle Keeley? You don't stand a chance in France!"

10

"Andrew used to be your friend," Kyle said to Miguel. "Maybe you could talk him into taking my place."

Kyle and Miguel were hanging out in the cafeteria, waiting for Sierra and Akimi to join them for their daily team meeting, something they'd been holding ever since Mr. Lemoncello announced his Library Olympics idea back in January.

"No way, bro," said Miguel. "We need you."

"No, you don't."

"You're our leader. *El capitán.*"

"But I shouldn't be. Sure, I know how to play games. But I'm still not great at all the library stuff."

"And I'm not very good at games," said Miguel. "And I haven't read half as many books as Sierra. And I'm nowhere near as clever as Akimi. The team needs all four of us, bro."

"But have you seen some of these kids in the regional competitions? They're amazing."

"Yeah. That girl Marjory up in Michigan sure knows her way around the stacks."

"That's why you guys need Andrew Peckleman. He used to be your second-in-command on the library squad."

"I already told you: Ever since he was booted out of the escape game, Andrew Peckleman does not like libraries. Besides, he can't practice with us after school, because he has a new job."

"What kind of job?" asked Kyle.

"He's working afternoons and weekends at the motel that opened up last month across from Liberty Park. Some distant relative that Andrew and his parents didn't even know they had owns the place. A great-uncle-twice-removed or something. He hired Andrew."

"Even though he's only twelve?"

Miguel shrugged. "I guess when it's family, it's different."

"What's Andrew do?"

"Sweeps. Makes sure the ice machine isn't clogged. Fills the bird feeders."

"Bird feeders?"

"What can I say? Andrew's uncle must love birds. He even named his motel the Blue Jay Extended Stay Lodge. Come on. Forget Andrew. We're counting on *you*."

That was the problem. Kyle didn't want to let his friends down. And he'd read Marjory Muldauer's interview with her hometown newspaper online.

42

She was gunning for Kyle.

Kyle *so* wished he could switch places with Andrew, even if it meant sweeping up birdseed.

He hadn't told any of his teammates, but in the six weeks since Mr. Lemoncello had announced his Library Olympic Games, Kyle felt a nervous fluttering in his stomach every time he played a board game against his brothers or fielded a riddle tossed at him by a school bus driver.

The pressure was intense.

Especially since Kyle had been on something of a losing streak—something else he hadn't told Miguel or Akimi or Sierra. He hadn't beaten his brothers on family game night *once* since January. Kyle had even lost the home version of the Escape from Mr. Lemoncello's Library board game—to his mom. And Miguel had been playing with Kyle that time. True, Miguel had given Kyle some bad advice. (*Flubber* is the name of a Walt Disney movie starring Robin Williams, not a book by Judy Blume, which would be *Blubber*.) But Kyle was the one who had given the wrong answer.

The first game in Mr. Lemoncello's library had been more like a scavenger hunt, something Kyle was good at. But these new Olympic Games were going to be about serious library topics, and Kyle would be playing against some serious library whiz kids.

Akimi and Sierra came into the otherwise empty cafeteria.

"Hey, guys," said Akimi. "Sorry we're late."

"Akimi was teaching me how to play that new Lemoncello video game where you squish all the different-colored jelly beans with a sledgehammer," said Sierra. "I made it to level three."

Kyle nodded. "Jujitsu Jelly Jam."

He didn't mention that he'd already made it to level fifty-three. Friends didn't gloat to friends.

"So what're we doing today?" asked Akimi. "More rebus puzzles? Dewey decimal drills?"

"First things first," said Miguel, jerking his thumb at Kyle. "Our fearless leader here is getting cold feet."

"Wha-hut?" said Akimi.

"Kyle wants to quit."

"I didn't say I want to quit, Miguel."

"Right. You just said you didn't want to be on the team anymore. That you wanted Andrew Peckleman to take your place."

"Which," said Akimi, "basically means you want to quit."

"I'm not a quitter," said Kyle.

"Uh, yes, if you quit, you are," said Akimi. "Sierra, correct me if I'm wrong."

"Sorry, Kyle," said Sierra. "That's the dictionary definition of 'quitter,' all right. 'A person who quits or gives up easily, especially in the face of some difficulty or danger.'"

"Snap," said Miguel. "Sierra just gave you the four-two-three on quitters."

Kyle was confused. "The what?"

44

"The four-two-three," said Akimi. "That's where you can always find a dictionary of standard English in a library."

"Oh," said Kyle. "Did not know that."

"It was on last week's study sheet," said Miguel.

"Right. Sorry. Guess I should've studied it."

"Well, duh," said Akimi. "That's why we call them *study* sheets."

Kyle pretended to laugh, but deep down, he knew the truth: No matter how hard he tried, he would never be able to win every single game he played for the rest of his life. Sometimes the cards and the dice and the questions just didn't go your way. Every chance for victory was another chance for defeat.

He didn't belong in anybody's Library Olympics.

11

Playing off the NCAA basketball tournament's "March Madness" theme, Mr. Lemoncello declared the first Saturday in March "Library Lunacy Day."

It was time for each of the seven regions to make its toughest cuts and choose the four members for its Library Olympics team.

At two p.m. Eastern Standard Time (eleven a.m. on the West Coast), Mr. Lemoncello himself addressed all the contestants via a video conference call. He wore a bright yellow shirt with a custom-cut tie shaped like a cello.

"Hearty and splendiferous congratulations on having made it this far in the competition. I wish I could invite each and every one of you *plus* everybody else in America to my first-ever Library Olympic Games, but, unfortunately, Ohio fire codes do not permit occupancy by more than three hundred and twenty-five million people, even if they are all little women. Good luck! Have fun! And remember, books are the true breakfast of champions! You may devour them. But please don't eat them. Thank you."

In California, where all sixteen finalists were library whizzes, Sarah Trager Logan, the librarian in charge, knew teamwork would be crucial for victory inside the Lemoncello Library. That's why she made all sixteen final-ists participate in a synchronized book-cart drill. It was judged by the same Hollywood celebrities who judge TV dancing shows.

In Colorado, the four members of the Mountain team would be the first four students who could solve one final puzzle. All the top contestants were given a sheet of paper with the following paragraph printed on it:

Thoze four beople who will represant awl of the bibrar-eans id the creat and heroik Mountain states knaw one thing aboot anything primted in a card cadalog sydtem. Without it, library users would simply be lost.

There were so many mistakes most of the contestants didn't know what it meant, what they were supposed to do, or why the judges hadn't proofread their paragraph before passing it around.

But the final four knew the mistakes *were* the secret code.

By writing down the letters that should have gone

where the wrong letters were, they came up with a simple lesson about library card catalogs:

SPELLING COUNTS.

In San Antonio, Texas, the final contest was a fresh and very complicated rebus puzzle.

"The category is 'famous quotes,'" said Cynthia Alaniz, the librarian who would be coaching the Southwest team. "Good luck!"

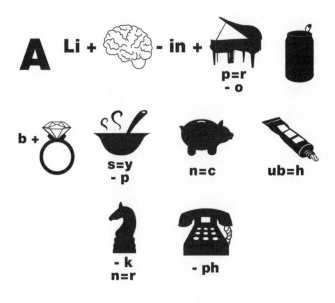

—Neil Gaiman

The eight finalists wrote their answers as quickly as they could. When they were finished, they put down their pencils and bopped bright yellow hotel bells.

The four fastest puzzle solvers nailed it: " 'Google can bring you back one hundred thousand answers. A librarian can bring you back the right one.' —Neil Gaiman"

Marjory Muldauer, who had aced every test and game thrown her way during the first eight rounds of the regional competition, was in Madison, Wisconsin, for the Midwest finals.

And she was feeling invincible.

In the Midwest's "elite eight," she played a rapid-fire "first lines" game.

A librarian stood at a podium and read from a note card. The contestants had to buzz in like they did on *Jeopardy!*

"'Where's Papa going with that axe?'" said the librarian.

Marjory slammed her fist down first.

BUZZ!

"*Charlotte's Web,* by E. B. White!"

"Correct. 'All children, except one, grow up.'"

Marjory banged her button.

BUZZ!

"*Peter Pan,* by J. M. Barrie!"

"Correct. 'In the light of the—'"

BUZZ!

Marjory didn't wait for the librarian to finish.

"*The Very Hungry Caterpillar,* by Eric Carle."

"Correct. 'Mrs. Rachel—'"

BUZZ!

"*Anne of Green Gables,* by L. M. Montgomery."

The other contestants never had a chance.

To lock down her spot on the four-person team, Marjory competed against five other finalists in one last Dewey decimal challenge.

"Give me the Dewey decimal number for 'freedom of speech,'" said Tabatha Otto, a librarian from Lincolnshire, Illinois.

Two contestants began weeping.

Three wrote down the same answer: 323.44.

"Very good," said the librarian.

"But not good enough," said Marjory. "Three-two-three-point-four-four is the call number for 'freedom of action,' also known as liberty. But three-two-three-point-four-four-*three* would be 'freedom of speech.' "

And that's what she had written on her card.

Marjory Muldauer was good.

Scary good.

12

On March 18, two days before the Library Olympic Games were scheduled to start, Mrs. Yunghans, the middle school librarian, showed Team Kyle a viral video of Marjory Muldauer's brilliant performance at the Midwest finals.

"Wow," said Akimi.

"Yikes," added Miguel. "She's amazing."

"She's also incredibly tall," said Akimi. "Like a praying mantis."

"She looks sort of sad," said Sierra.

Kyle didn't say a word.

This was the last straw.

Seeing Marjory Muldauer in action, watching her guess first sentences of books with just one or two words for a clue, Kyle knew he didn't stand a chance. Not against that kind of competition. The girl knew Dewey decimal codes down to the one-thousandths place. Kyle still wasn't sure what "the four-two-three" meant.

Plus, the Lemoncello Library had been closed to the public for a week. Mysterious imagineers from Mr. Lemoncello's headquarters in New York City had come to Alexandriaville to make what the local newspaper called "a few minor alterations." They'd been working inside the locked building under the supervision of Dr. Zinchenko, adding new surprises for the Olympic Games.

Surprises Kyle knew would totally baffle him.

He would go into the Lemoncello Library a champion and come out a chump. There would be no more cake days.

It wasn't so much that Kyle was afraid of losing (even though he was). He didn't want to be the reason everybody else lost, too.

"What kind of new gadgets and gizmos do you guys think Mr. Lemoncello has added to his library?" asked Mrs. Yunghans.

"It's top-secret," said Miguel.

"Nobody knows," added Akimi.

"Probably not even Mr. Lemoncello," said Sierra.

Once again, Kyle remained silent.

"I guess all we can do now to prep is read more books," said Miguel.

But the books would have to come from the middle school media center. The week the library was closed for its "alterations," nobody could check out books, which made the League of Concerned Library Lovers very upset.

"A public library should serve *the public*," said Charles Chiltington's mother on the radio and TV. "Not the whims of an eccentric billionaire."

Fortunately, nobody in Alexandriaville paid much attention to Mrs. Chiltington or her group. They were too excited about the upcoming Library Olympics. All the local hotels and motels lit their "No Vacancies" neons. Restaurants hired more staff. Mr. Lemoncello's wacky idea was an economic boon for the whole town.

The opening ceremonies were scheduled for the first day of spring, March 20. The twelve games of the duodecimalthon would start on the twenty-first and run for six days (two games a day). Closing ceremonies would take place the following night.

The public was invited to attend and watch. For free. The games would also be broadcast on many PBS stations, the Book Network cable channel, and NPR.

That meant everybody in America would be able to watch and/or listen to Marjory Muldauer destroy Kyle Keeley, big-time.

The Alexandriaville four, as well as the seven visiting teams, their coaches, and tutors (so they could keep up with their schoolwork for the week) would be staying at what Mr. Lemoncello had dubbed Olympia Village. It was actually the Blue Jay Extended Stay Lodge, where Andrew Peckleman had a part-time job.

And that's where Kyle was headed—as soon as Mrs. Yunghans wrapped up this final team meeting.

"You guys have done a great job," said the school librarian. "And, Kyle? We're all very glad you're still on the team."

"Thanks."

"Yo, Kyle," said Miguel, "don't let this Marjory Muldauer get under your dome. We can take her."

"You're not thinking about quitting again, are you?" asked Akimi.

That was the problem with best friends. They knew what you were thinking even when you were pretending not to be thinking it.

"I'm fine," said Kyle. "Just, you know, nervous."

"I think we all are," said Mrs. Yunghans, who'd be staying with the team at Olympia Village as one of their chaperones. "Look, guys—tomorrow's Saturday. I think we should all take a break. No more studying. No games. Just head over to Liberty Park, take in some fresh air, and don't read anything."

Sierra raised her hand. "Is that an order, Mrs. Yunghans?"

"No, Sierra. You can read if you want to. But read something for yourself—not the competition."

Kyle said goodbye to his friends, and when he was absolutely certain nobody was following him, he biked to the Blue Jay Extended Stay Lodge.

He needed to talk to Andrew Peckleman now—*before* Marjory Muldauer came to town.

13

The motel's sign looked like a big blue birdhouse.

The reader board out front, where the letters used to say "Ask About Our Early-Bird Specials," now read "Welcome to Olympia Village."

Kyle checked out the property. It looked like an apartment complex, with maybe a dozen or so two-story structures and parking lots spreading out in either direction from a central building that had a lobby, a dining room, and an office.

There was also a ton of bird feeders. Everywhere. Birdbaths and birdhouses, too.

Andrew Peckleman was working near the motel sign, pouring a sack of birdseed into one of the feeders. Kyle biked over to talk to him.

"Hey, Andrew."

"Kyle."

"So. Sunday's the big day."

"For what?"

"The Library Olympics."

"Oh, right."

"I was wondering . . ."

Before Kyle could say another word, a black SUV crawled to a stop behind him. One of the rear doors swung open, and out stepped Charles Chiltington.

"I'll only be a second, Mummy," Chiltington said to someone in the backseat. Kyle squinted at the tinted front windshield. The Chiltingtons had a chauffeur. The guy was even wearing one of those floppy black hats with the shiny brim.

"Hello, Keeley," said Charles, who never called Kyle by his first name (probably because "Keeley" made him sound more like a servant).

"Hey, Charles," said Kyle.

"What are you doing here?" asked Andrew.

"Following Keeley."

Andrew looked confused. "Why?"

"Because I knew that, sooner or later, he would come here and beg you to take his place in the Library Olympics."

Kyle faked a chuckle. "What?"

"My mother and I have been enjoying the regional competitions," said Charles. "You don't stand a chance against that Marjory Muldauer girl, Keeley. I know it. You know it. The whole country knows it. And since Mr. Lemoncello is so eager to let Andrew back in the game . . ."

"He is?" said Andrew. "Where'd you hear that?"

"I have my spies," said Charles.

"Spies?" Kyle said with a laugh. "Mr. Lemoncello was talking about you back in January, Andrew. When he first announced his idea for these Olympics. He knows you were bullied into stealing Sierra's card during the escape game. He'd really like to have you come back to his library."

"Well, I won't do it," whined Peckleman, pushing his goggle-sized glasses up the bridge of his nose. "Mr. Lemoncello is stupid. His whole library is stupid. And Library Olympics? That's the stupidest idea I've ever heard. You're wasting your time, Kyle. I won't take your place."

"Who said that's why I'm here?" asked Kyle.

Andrew pointed at Charles. "He did."

"Look, Keeley, *I'll* take your place," said Charles. "Mummy and her group are keen to have me on the inside, keeping an eye on Mr. Lemoncello. Besides, who knows? I might be able to whip your atrocious teammates into shape. With me at the helm, we could actually bring home the gold." He stood proudly, looking down his nose at Kyle. "Do I need to fill out a form or something?"

"For what?"

Charles rolled his eyes. "*To take your place.* We all know that's why you came here, Keeley. You're afraid. Abashed. Apprehensive. Frankly, I don't blame you. You're a loser who got lucky. Once. I, on the other hand, am a Chiltington. Chiltingtons never lose."

58

"Except when you lost," said Andrew, nervously fidgeting with his glasses. "You know. Last time."

"I did not 'lose,' Andrew. I was *eliminated* by Mr. Lemoncello."

Kyle shook his head. "I hate to disappoint you and your 'mummy,' Charles, but I didn't come here to ask Andrew to take my place."

"Oh, really?"

"Nope. And I sure don't want you anywhere near Akimi, Miguel, and Sierra. I just wanted to make sure Andrew saved Miguel and me a good room. We're checking in Sunday afternoon."

"What?" said Charles. "You're not quitting."

"Nope. Just wanted to check out our accommodations. Haven't you heard, Charles? Winners never quit, and quitters never win."

14

The next day, when Kyle and his teammates were dropped off at Olympia Village by their parents, the motel was swarming with kids and chaperones.

"Uh-oh," said Akimi. "They all have slick warm-up outfits."

The seven other teams were decked out in brightly colored hoodies and sweatpants. Kyle and his friends were wearing jeans, sneakers, and mismatched jackets. So were their chaperones.

"That's okay," said Sierra. "We're saving our uniforms for the parade of champions."

"Check it out, you guys," said Miguel. "There's Andrew Peckleman."

Their classmate marched briskly out of the hotel lobby wearing a bright blue sweatshirt and a Toronto Blue Jays baseball cap.

"May I have your attention, please?" Andrew shouted through a bullhorn. "May I have your attention?"

No one gave him any attention.

All the kids from out of state and their chaperones kept gabbing and giggling.

"So when do we get to check out this Lemoncello Library?" said a boy with the kind of tough edge New Yorkers always have in movies.

"I sure do want to ride one of those hover ladders," said a girl who sounded like she might be from Alabama or Louisiana.

"Dude," said a kid from California, "I'm heading straight to the Electronic Learning Center so I can half-pipe the craters on the moon."

Andrew tried again. His bullhorn squealed with feedback. "WILL YOU STUPID PEOPLE PLEASE SHUT UP?"

Every single Library Olympian glared at him.

"Thank you. Um, now, here with a few words about the motel is my boss and, uh, great-uncle-twice-removed, Mr. Woodrow 'Woody' Peckleman."

A skinny bald man—who sort of resembled a plucked chicken in a bright blue suit—strutted out the lobby door. He had a very pointy nose that looked like a beak. He twitched and fidgeted and squinted in the sunshine. Kyle half expected him to start scratching the toe of his shoe at the dirt, searching for chicken feed.

"Welcome," said Mr. Peckleman, with a voice even

more nasal than Andrew's. "The Blue Jay Extended Stay Lodge—also known, this week, as Olympia Village—is, as you may have noticed, my personal bird sanctuary. Please enjoy our feathered friends' colorful, song-filled company and merry antics." He gestured toward a nearby bird feeder. "But, please, do *not* feed the squirrels. Squirrels are nothing but thieving rodents. Rats with fluffy tails."

Oh-kay, Kyle thought. *Andrew's great-uncle is a little nutty.*

"Also," Mr. Peckleman continued, "you are free to enjoy the brand-new Lemoncello video arcade machines recently installed in the motel's game room, right off the lobby. There is no charge for any of these games."

"Woo-hoo," cried Kyle.

Now everybody in the crowd turned to gawk at him.

Right. Kyle figured his competition was more into books and libraries than video games. He felt as out of place as he'd known he would.

"That's okay," whispered Akimi. "I'll play Dragon Bop Bubble Pop with you."

"Me too," added Sierra.

"Ditto," tossed in Miguel.

"Thanks, you guys."

Suddenly, an old-fashioned horn went *AH-OOGA.*

Kyle looked at the motel entrance.

A car resembling a pouncing cat, with glowing green eyeballs for headlights, had just eased off the highway and pulled into the parking lot.

"The cat is one of the tokens from that board game," said Sierra, who had been studying Lemoncello games the way Kyle had been studying libraries and books. "Family Frenzy!"

"Correctamundo," said Akimi.

The cat car was followed by eight Winnebago-sized vehicles, their sides covered with vinyl graphics designed to make them look like bookshelves on wheels.

"And check those out," said Miguel as the vehicles gracefully glided into a reserved row of angled parking spaces.

The catmobile's paw door swung up, and out stepped Dr. Yanina Zinchenko, wearing a blazing-red flight suit. She strode through the crowd and politely took the bullhorn from Mr. Peckleman.

"Welcome, everybody, to Ohio and Olympia Village," she said. "Kindly report to the bookmobile with your region's name affixed to its side. Our library staff will give each of you a welcome packet containing the card key for your room, meal tickets, and information about this week's exciting events. The bookmobiles will be at your disposal throughout the games. They will take you wherever you need to go. They are also filled with books to make your commute more enjoyable. The opening ceremonies for the games of the first Library Olympiad will be held this evening, here at Olympia Village. Start time is eight p.m. There will be fireworks. And cake. Also balloons. So please, settle in, freshen up, and get ready for an exciting week."

Everyone applauded. Dr. Zinchenko clicked her heels and bowed.

Two smiling Lemoncello Library staffers in yellow jumpsuits with ID badges lanyarded around their necks emerged from each of the eight bookmobiles with stacks of manila envelopes.

"Let's go get our room assignments," said Mrs. Yunghans, the middle school librarian. Mr. Colby Sharp, one of the middle school's ELA teachers, would be Team Kyle's other chaperone.

Kyle, Akimi, Miguel, and Sierra followed the two adults to the bookmobile with "Home Team/Defending Champions" proudly displayed on its side.

The gangly Marjory Muldauer was standing with the two yellow-suited library staffers in front of it.

"Excuse me, Miss Muldauer," said Mrs. Yunghans, who of course recognized the girl immediately. "Are you looking for the Midwest team's bookmobile?"

"No," said Marjory. "I was just curious if any of the reigning 'champions' knew when the first perambulating library appeared in the rural villages of Cumbria County, England."

Kyle looked to Miguel and Sierra. They looked blankly at him.

"The first what?" said Akimi.

"Perambulating library." Marjory gestured over her shoulder. "A bookmobile. A mobile library?"

"Is this going to be on the final?" quipped Kyle. He was

64

trying his best to sound confident in front of his fiercest rival.

Marjory Muldauer kept her eyes locked on Kyle. "You never know, do you, Mr. Keeley?"

"Miss Muldauer," said Mrs. Yunghans, "perhaps you should rejoin the rest of your team?"

Marjory ignored her.

"It was 1857," she said. "It was a horse-drawn cart. Donated by a Victorian merchant named George Moore to 'diffuse good literature among the rural population.'"

"Well," said Kyle, "these are way cooler. And the drivers don't have to shovel horse poop all day."

Marjory Muldauer didn't laugh. She narrowed her eyes.

"I hope you enjoyed your fifteen minutes of fame, Mr. Keeley. Because when these games are over and done, *you* will be over and done, too."

She turned on her heel and walked away. Kyle actually shivered.

The girl wasn't just scary good. She was also scary.

15

Andrew Peckleman was in the motel game room.

"For the last time, the stupid thing is broken," he told the blond boy from Utah, who was on the Mountain team.

"How can it be broken? The motel manager said all these games are brand-new."

"Well, maybe Mr. Lemoncello made a lemon." Andrew jiggled the control knobs on the console. He jabbed his thumb at the on/off button. Finally, he gave the pressboard box a swift kick. "See? It doesn't work. Play something else."

"But I wanted to play Squirrel Squad Six."

"And I wanted to be the first librarian on Mars. Ask me how that's working out. Now go play something else."

The boy from Utah shuffled off to try Mr. Lemoncello's Disgracefully Destructive Elephant Stampede. The goal was to mash as much mall merchandise as you could with Melvin, the mischievous mastodon.

"Andrew?" called his uncle from the motel's front office.

"Yes, sir, Uncle Woody?"

"Come here, please."

Andrew stepped into the office. His uncle was at the back wall, fiddling with the combination lock on a large steel door.

"I'll just be a minute." He slid a rolling wall panel in front of the steel door. When the panel clicked into place, the massive storage locker was completely hidden behind a seamless wall featuring a framed print of two bluebirds.

Andrew's uncle pointed to a thirty-pound sack of birdseed sitting on the floor.

"I need you to refill feeders six and seven."

"Yes, sir."

"And check the batteries in the spinners."

"Yes, sir."

Each of Uncle Woody's bird feeders had a weight-activated spinner that turned it into a whirling merry-go-round the instant a squirrel set foot on it.

"I need to go chat with a few of our guests."

"About what?" asked Andrew.

"Never you mind. Go take care of the bird feeders."

"Yes, sir."

Lugging the seed bag over his shoulder, Andrew went out the side door to the swimming pool and patio area.

Since it was only the first day of spring, the pool was still covered with a tarp, but the stainless steel gas grills on the concrete slab surrounding it had been shined and buffed. Cooks from a catering company would use them for the opening ceremonies celebration. Hamburgers, hot dogs, and s'mores were on the menu.

The outdoor fire pit—an elevated ring of rocks surrounded by lawn chairs—was stone cold. It would not be lit at any time during the Library Olympic Games because Mr. Lemoncello hated bonfires. "Throughout history," he explained in the Library Olympics welcome packet, "too many books have been burned by people who didn't like what was written inside them."

There would also be no flaming Olympic torch, just a giant, ten-foot-tall flashlight to celebrate the joy of reading under the covers. It was mounted on the back of a flatbed truck and would swing through the sky after Mr. Lemoncello switched it on, just like one of those swiveling spotlights at the grand opening of a used-car dealership.

Andrew unscrewed a cap on bird feeder number six and hoisted the bag of seed.

"Why does this hotel have so many bird feeders?" asked someone behind him.

Andrew whirled around.

It was the tall girl from Michigan. Marjory Muldauer.

Andrew adjusted his glasses. "Excuse me?"

"What's up with all the bird feeders?"

Andrew shrugged. "Uncle Woody likes birds."

"Probably because he looks like a bird."

Andrew snorted a laugh. "I know. He does!"

"I'm trying to find some coffee," said Marjory, her hands propped on her hips. Her face was scrunched up like she'd just smelled sour milk. "I need to read two more books tonight."

"Well," said Andrew, "if you really want some 641.3373, follow me."

Marjory gave him a look. "That's the Dewey decimal number for coffee."

"Yes. The beverage. Coffee the agricultural product would be 633.73."

"And," said Marjory, "coffee*houses* would be 647.95. Eating and drinking establishments."

"Yep."

"You know a lot about the Dewey decimal system for a motel employee."

"Oh, this is just a part-time job. My name is Andrew. Andrew Peckleman."

"You were one of the losers, weren't you? In the escape game."

Andrew hung his head in shame. "Yes. But ask me if I care."

"Okay," said Marjory. "Do you care?"

"No. Not anymore."

"Well, that monstrosity that Mr. Lemoncello constructed isn't really a library, Andrew. It's an indoor amusement park."

"Have you seen it?" Andrew asked.

"Not yet. But I've seen pictures. They should close

it down and turn it into a Chuck E. Cheese's—after, of course, I win my college scholarship from loony old Lemoncello."

Andrew smiled.

Because Marjory Muldauer was a kindred spirit.

He dropped the birdseed sack onto the concrete patio.

"Come on," he said. "Let's go grab that cup of 641.3373."

"And maybe," said Marjory, "we can find a few 641.8653 to go with it."

"Ooh," said Andrew. "I love doughnuts."

16

Just after dark, Kyle and his teammates put on their opening ceremonies costumes and headed out to the motel's central courtyard.

A bandstand had been erected at one end of the grassy rectangle situated in the middle of the motel's chalet-style units. Mr. Lemoncello, Dr. Zinchenko, and the mayor of Alexandriaville stood on the platform, ready to review the thirty-two Olympians.

Mr. Lemoncello was dressed in a shimmering silver toga and silver laurel-leaf crown. He looked a little like the male tribute from District Three in a *Hunger Games* parade. Dr. Zinchenko was all in red, again. Shiny red sequins. The mayor wore a black trench coat. He wasn't much on dressing up.

The eight teams marched, one at a time, into the motel's version of an arena and walked around it, just like the athletes at the ancient Greek Olympic Games did (except those guys didn't have a sidewalk or running shoes).

A crowd of several hundred spectators ringed the courtyard, which was illuminated by colorful strings of party lights. More people were watching the festivities on giant-screen TVs set up across the highway in Liberty Park.

Kyle was carrying the "Hometown Heroes" banner. He and his teammates were wearing gray-and-scarlet tracksuits (Ohio State University's colors), brown "buckeye" nut hats, and squeaking banana shoes, exactly like the ones Mr. Lemoncello sometimes wore. The musical sneakers—bright yellow and slightly curved—were one of Mr. Lemoncello's biggest hits over the holidays. The "game" was to make the banana shoes burp-squeak out a tune by hopping, skipping, and tap-dancing the notes. For the opening ceremonies' "Parade of Champions," Kyle, Akimi, Miguel, and Sierra had choreographed the footwork to play a burp-squeak version of "Hang On Sloopy," Ohio's official rock song.

Most of the other teams wore wacky costumes, too.

The team from the Pacific states was decked out in board shorts, flip-flops, and way cool Hawaiian shirts. They blew "Surfin' Safari" on kazoos. Pranav Pillai was the kazoo drum major.

The kids representing the Mid-Atlantic region wore crab costumes, complete with deely-bopper antennae and pinchers.

The Northeasterners went with very scholarly, Harry

Potter–style robes and mumbled a chant in Latin while they marched (*"Semper ubi sub ubi"*); the Southeast team, including Diane Capriola, wore sleek NASCAR race car driver jumpsuits with all sorts of book patches sewn onto every available inch; the Southwest team sported cowboy hats, big belt buckles, and boots and did rope tricks with their twirling lassoes; all the Mountain players wore flannel shirts, lumberjack pants, fake mountain-man beards (even the girls), and furry, flap-eared hats.

The Midwest team, led by Marjory Muldauer, wore khaki pants, button-down white shirts, striped ties, and blue blazers.

Kyle thought the Midwesterners looked like marching real-estate brokers. Or Charles Chiltington's cousins.

"My dad made it!" said Sierra, waving at a man smiling proudly in the crowd. "And there's my mom," she added when the team had hop-skipped and burp-squeaked another twenty feet.

After all eight teams had marched around the courtyard three times, they lined up in front of Mr. Lemoncello's reviewing stand, ready for him to officially declare the games open and light the Library Olympics torch, which, Sierra explained, is what people in England call a flashlight.

"Welcome, one and all," boomed Mr. Lemoncello. "I am so glad to see you here this evening, because this afternoon my optometrist gave me eye drops and I couldn't see a thing! Before I officially illuminate our Olympic torch . . ."

He gestured toward the ten-foot-tall skyward-pointing flashlight.

"... I'd like to say a few short words. 'Terse,' 'diminutive,' 'stubby,' and 'I,' which is one of the shortest words I know, until it becomes 'we,' as in 'We the people of the United States,' the same 'we' that secured the blessings of liberty for ourselves and our posterity, which, by the way, would be you, children, and not my fanny, which would, of course, be my 'posterior-ity.'"

He took a deep breath.

"Tonight, we light the symbolic flashlight of under-the-covers reading to celebrate those page-turners we can never put down, even on a school night. I am assured that our Olympic torch will never reach a temperature of Fahrenheit four fifty-one, something the Lorax, the lion, the witch, and the wardrobe were all quite happy to hear."

Mr. Lemoncello pranced across the stage to a giant cartoon version of a wall switch.

"Gamesters, if you're game, let the gaming begin!" He heaved up the humongous switch. The ginormous flashlight's beacon sliced through the night sky. "I now pronounce the games of the first Library Olympiad officially open. I also pronounce my name like a cross between a tart fruit and a mellow musical instrument. Have fun! Play fair! And remember—these games are a quest to find who amongst you is a true champion!"

A thousand balloons with glow sticks in their bellies were released into the night air. Fireworks rocketed into the sky. The Ohio State marching band tramped into the courtyard to create an open-book formation while blaring a brassy version of "Paperback Writer" by the Beatles. Laser beams sliced through the smoky darkness in time to the music.

"And now," announced Mr. Lemoncello after the fireworks had exploded into their grand finale of floating hearts, smiley faces, and interlocking books, "the most stupendously spectacular moment of the entire night, your keys to anything and everything you ever want or need to know, boys and girls, buoys and gulls, dolphins and porpoises—may I proudly present . . . your library cards!"

17

The eight teams stood bunched in front of the reviewing stand.

Dr. Zinchenko called out names one by one.

Kyle and his friends would be last to receive their new, Olympic-edition library cards. It was like baseball. The home team always batted last.

Miguel nudged Kyle. "You think there's going to be another secret, coded clue on the back of the cards?"

When Kyle and his teammates had played the escape game, one of their biggest clues came from writing down the first letters of all the books printed on the backs of their library cards. The letters spelled out a sentence that pointed them toward the library's secret exit.

"I hope so," said Akimi. "Because none of the other teams will know how to play Mr. Lemoncello's First Letters game."

"Maybe we should tell them," suggested Sierra.

"Why?" asked Akimi. "I thought we wanted to win."

"We do," said Sierra. "But we don't want to cheat."

"Yo," said Miguel. "It's not cheating just because we know something the other teams don't."

Sierra sighed. "But it's an unfair advantage."

"True," said Akimi. "But, sometimes, those are my favorite kind."

"But remember Mr. Lemoncello's motto?" said Sierra. " 'Knowledge not shared remains unknown.' "

"Which," said Akimi, "is exactly how I want this particular piece of knowledge to remain: unknown to everybody except us!"

"You guys?" said Kyle as the line worked its way forward. "Let's wait and see. I'd be surprised if Mr. Lemoncello gave us the same kind of clue twice. He never does it in his board games."

Finally, Team Kyle's names were called.

Dr. Zinchenko handed them four cards.

"Your library cards will grant you access to all the rooms and areas where we will be playing our twelve games," she explained. "The winner of each game will receive a very special medal. The team with the most medals at the end of the week will be declared the winner, if not the champion."

"Huh?" said Miguel. "Isn't the winner automatically the champion?"

"Perhaps," Dr. Zinchenko said mysteriously. "Perhaps not. It all depends, don't you agree?"

Miguel shrugged. "I guess."

Kyle wasn't paying attention to Dr. Zinchenko. He was too focused on the fact that the library cards were, once again, numbered.

"Now, if you children will excuse me . . . ," said Dr. Zinchenko, touching her Bluetooth earpiece. "It seems Mr. Lemoncello needs me inside. He has glued his mouth shut on a caramel apple."

Dr. Zinchenko hurried into the motel.

The players on the seven other teams had already headed into the dining area off the lobby, where waiters were serving hamburgers, hot dogs, potato chips, s'mores, ice cream, cake, candy bars, cookies, caramel apples, and coconut cream pie. "There is also fruit," Mr. Lemoncello had announced, "for those who do not wish to be bouncing off the walls all night, as I will be."

Team Kyle's chaperones, Mrs. Yunghans and Mr. Sharp, came over to join them.

"Good job on the parade, you guys," said Mrs. Yunghans. "We're going inside to grab one of those burgers."

"We're right behind you," said Kyle.

"Totally," added Miguel.

The four teammates waited.

As soon as the adults were gone, they flipped over their library cards.

There were images of book covers printed on the back.

"Awesome," said Akimi. "Just like last time. You guys know the drill. We need to write down the first letters of every title."

"I've got a pen and some paper," said Sierra, digging into the hip pocket of her tracksuit.

The team laid down their cards in order. Two cards had three illustrated book covers on their backs; two cards had four:

CARD #1

The Candymakers by Wendy Mass

Holes by Louis Sachar

Inside Out and Back Again by Thanhha Lai

CARD #2

Splendors and Glooms by Laura Amy Schlitz

Incident at Hawk's Hill by Allan W. Eckert

Shabanu: Daughter of the Wind by Suzanne Fisher Staples

Nothing but the Truth: A Documentary Novel by Avi

CARD #3

One Came Home by Amy Timberlake

The Year of Billy Miller by Kevin Henkes

A Long Way from Chicago by Richard Peck

Criss Cross by Lynne Rae Perkins

CARD #4

Lizzie Bright and the Buckminster Boy by Gary D. Schmidt

Uncle Tom's Cabin by Harriet Beecher Stowe

Elijah of Buxton by Christopher Paul Curtis

"Okay," said Kyle. "That's T-H-I, S-I-S-N, O-T-A-C, L-U-E."

Miguel gave it a quick shot. "Thigh, sis, 'n' taco, Lou!"

"Whuh?" said Akimi.

"It's like you're at KFC and you're ordering some Original Recipe dark meat plus a taco for your sister, Louise. Or maybe you know the guy behind the counter and his name is Lou."

Akimi rolled her eyes. "Seriously, Miguel? They don't serve tacos at KFC."

"Yes, they do if it's a KFC–Taco Bell combo store, which sometimes they are."

"I don't think the First Letters game is going to work for us this time," said Sierra.

She showed them what she had written down on her slip of paper:

"This is not a clue."

"Oh," said Miguel. "Did not see that coming."

Kyle, on the other hand, sort of had.

He knew *nothing* about winning these Olympic Games would be easy.

Bright and early the next morning, Kyle, his teammates, and their chaperones climbed into their bookmobile for the drive downtown to the Lemoncello Library.

The adults sat up front with the driver.

The kids were in the back with the books and a mini-fridge stocked with chocolate milk, pop, and six different kinds of juice.

"So," said Miguel, "did Andrew's weird uncle talk to any of you guys last night?"

"He talked to me this morning," said Sierra. "When I was on my way to the breakfast room."

"What did he want?" asked Kyle.

"He told me he could give me a 'Go to College Free' card," said Sierra.

Miguel nodded. "Me too."

"And why wasn't I offered this card?" asked Akimi.

Miguel shrugged. "Maybe because I turned him down."

"So did I," said Sierra.

"What did he want in exchange for the card?" asked Kyle.

"Worms for his baby birds?" suggested Akimi.

"He didn't really say," replied Miguel. "I turned him down before he had a chance."

"Me too," said Sierra. "I also reminded him that winning a college scholarship isn't the only reason we're playing these games."

"Really?" said Akimi, arching an eyebrow. "What other reason is there?"

"To prove that we truly deserve to be crowned champions."

"Oh. Right. *That*."

"This could be part of the game," said Kyle.

"Seriously?" said Akimi.

"Yep. Mr. Peckleman is kind of working for Mr. Lemoncello this week—running Olympia Village. And in Mr. Lemoncello's Marvelously Mysterious Mine Shaft game, there are devious dwarves who offer you cheat cards that let you do stuff like use elf shovels even if you're not an elf. But elf shovels, you find out after it's too late, can't dig up diamonds, only gold, and you need a ton of gold plus two diamonds to win."

Sierra nodded very slowly. "You've played a lot of Mr. Lemoncello's games, haven't you, Kyle?"

"Enough to know that most of his cheat cards eventually come back to bite you in the butt."

When Kyle and his teammates entered the library's grand rotunda, the room was more crowded than they had ever seen it.

Spectators, staring up at the Wonder Dome, were seated at the four rings of tables. The players from the seven other teams milled around, *ooh*ing and *aah*ing at things Kyle and his friends now took for granted, like the holographic statues perched on their pedestals, peering down at the crowd below. The statues were waving at people who were waving up at them.

Kyle recognized only one of the projected images—a greenish bald guy wearing bifocals and pants cut off at the knees and tugging on a kite string. That had to be Benjamin Franklin.

"Who are those other people?" he whispered.

"Famous librarians," said Miguel. "Melvil Dewey, Eratosthenes, Saint Lawrence, Lewis Carroll—the usual suspects."

Kyle nodded. He was *so glad* Miguel was on his team.

"In honor of the ancient Olympic Games," reported Akimi, "they have all sorts of Grecian urns up in the Art and Artifacts Room. And you can check out Mr. Lemoncello's old gym shoes in the Lemoncello-abilia Room on the third floor. Bring a gas mask."

"I heard Muhammad Ali is boxing Rocky Balboa in

the IMAX theater," added Miguel. "Winner wrestles Hercules."

Up on the Wonder Dome screens, Kyle saw the enormous image of eight empty library carts and two rolling bins bulging with books. They seemed to be parked in front of the doors to the 000s Dewey decimal room on the second floor.

"Welcome, children!" cried a trembling voice. "I'm so glad you are all finally here! What took you so long?"

Kyle looked toward the circulation desk in the center of the round room. Usually, that was where Dr. Zinchenko and her staff worked, helping people find whatever information or books they were looking for. During the escape game, a holographic version of Mr. Lemoncello's favorite childhood librarian, Mrs. Gail Tobin, had popped in to help administer clues.

Today's guest-librarian hologram, the lady with the trembling voice, was somebody new.

She looked frazzled. Worn out. The way teachers sometimes look at the end of a really long day right before spring break.

"My name is Lonni Gause," said the shaky see-through librarian. She was nervously nibbling a pencil as though it were a cob of corn. "I was the very last librarian at the old Alexandriaville Public Library—the one they bulldozed down so they could build a parking garage." She started sobbing. "Oh, the horror! The horror!"

"Thank you, Mrs. Gause," said Dr. Zinchenko, striding into the room from a section of the fiction bookshelves that swung open like a hidden passageway in a castle. "Welcome to day one of our competition, Library Olympians. Today we begin our quest for champions!"

"Yes!" cried the holographic librarian. "We need champions. We also need defenders! We needed them all those years ago when, first, books started disappearing off the shelves and, then, the wrecking balls rumbled up Main Street. Oh, the horror. The horror!"

Dr. Zinchenko pointed and clicked a miniature remote at the wailing librarian. The librarian disappeared.

"Perhaps we'll hear more from Mrs. Gause. Later. Now, however, it is time for our first game. Will all thirty-two contestants please report to the second-floor balcony? Spectators? You may witness the event, live and in high-definition color, up on the Wonder Dome."

"This way, you guys," Kyle said to the kids from out of town as he headed toward the nearest spiral staircase. All the Library Olympians followed and clomped up the metal steps.

"Kindly report to your assigned library cart," said a soothing female voice oozing out of the second floor's ceiling speakers. "And remember, free people read freely."

Marjory Muldauer, walking with her Midwest teammates, chuffed a sarcastic laugh. "Thanks for the sappy bumper sticker, ceiling lady."

The second floor was a carpeted, circular balcony, with the same circumference as the Rotunda Reading Room below. The twelve-foot-wide balcony was lined with evenly spaced massive wooden doors that opened up into the ten Dewey decimal rooms.

Eight library carts—three tiers of slanted shelves on wheels—were lined up in front of the door to the 000s room. Across from them stood two canvas bins, both loaded with books.

Each library cart was labeled with two laminated cards: one with the name of a team, the other designating a range of Dewey decimal numbers. The Hometown Heroes' empty cart was labeled "900–999."

"That's for history and geography," Miguel reminded Kyle.

"Welcome to our first event: the Library Cart Relay Race," said Dr. Zinchenko, coming through another secret panel. This one was cut into the back of the curved fiction bookcases, which climbed past the second floor on their way up to the dome. "To win this game, your team must be the first to complete four laps of the second-floor balcony without spilling any of the three dozen books stacked on your rolling shelves, no matter the obstacles."

Marjory Muldauer's arm shot up.

"Yes?" said Dr. Zinchenko.

"There aren't any books on the library carts."

"No? Oh, that's right. The library has been closed for a week, so all of the recently returned books—exactly two hundred and eighty-eight different titles, thirty-six from each of eight different Dewey categories—are presently stored in one of those two rolling bins. You must find the books that belong in your group, carefully load your cart, and, then, each team member must complete one full lap of the balcony and cleanly pass the cart off to the next relay racer. The team that finishes first will take home today's first medal and move closer to their college scholarships. I suggest choosing your swiftest cart pusher for the final leg."

"That's you, Akimi," said Kyle. "You're the fastest."

"I'm the slowest," said Miguel.

"I'm pretty slow, too," added Sierra. "I'm more of a reader than a racer."

"That's okay," said Kyle. "You two will be in charge of finding our books for us."

"The numbers should be on the spine," said Miguel. "Look for anything that starts with a nine."

"By the way," said Dr. Zinchenko, "to make this game more challenging, we have temporarily covered up all the call numbers on the spines of the books in the bins."

"Oh-kay," said Akimi. "So much for that idea."

"Find books about historical events and places you've always wanted to visit," suggested Sierra.

"How about the bathroom?" said Kyle, feeling queasy. "I wouldn't mind visiting it right now."

"Relax, bro," said Miguel. "Sierra and I will load the cart. You and Akimi need to run real fast once it's good to go."

"You take the first leg," said Akimi. "Try to buy us an early lead."

Kyle nodded. He was pretty swift. Not as fast as Akimi, but thanks to his big brother Mike the Jock, he was used to running wind sprints. "I'll give it my best shot."

"Please stand by," said the soothing ceiling voice. "Once your cart is fully loaded, do not block, trip, or shove the other teams. Do not interfere with their cart handoffs."

"In other words," said a new voice in the ceiling—Mr. Lemoncello's—"play nice, cart runners—not to be confused with kite runners, a book you should all definitely read when you're a little older. Dr. Zinchenko? Let the book-sorting shindig begin!"

Dr. Zinchenko raised her arm. She was holding a fancy tasseled bookmark between her fingers as if it were a small flag.

"On your mark," she said. "Get set. Go!"

She lowered the bookmark.

The race was on!

19

Kyle and Akimi hung back while Sierra and Miguel dug through the book bins with a couple dozen other eager Dewey decimal decoders.

A short, scrappy kid from the Southeast team leapt into one of the rolling canvas containers and tossed out language books (the 400s) to his teammates.

Marjory Muldauer simply stood next to the book heaps and pointed. "That one. That one. That one, too."

"That's our first twelve!" said Miguel when he and Sierra filled the lowest shelf of the library cart with their first two armloads of books. "Only two dozen more to go!"

If somebody put a wrong book on a cart, the lady in the ceiling said, "Sorry, Northeast team," or "Sorry, Pacific team." Then she urged them to "please try again."

Sierra and Miguel didn't make a single mistake. Neither did Marjory Muldauer.

The guys from the Pacific and Northeast teams goofed up the most. They kept mixing up their 100s (philosophy and psychology) with their 200s (religion).

"Go!" said Miguel, loading the thirty-sixth book about history and geography onto Team Kyle's cart.

Kyle took off at the exact same second as the first relay racer for Marjory Muldauer's Midwest team.

The front left wheel on Kyle's rumbling three-tiered wagon was wobbly. Like a grocery cart with a squished grape stuck to one of its tires.

The whole library cart was shimmying.

But he didn't slow down.

After he passed through the tunnel behind the fiction shelves and hit the doors to the 300s room, he was in the lead.

He aimed for the inside railing, figuring the tighter the circle he ran, the faster he'd complete his lap.

Pranav Pillai from the Pacific team came tearing up on his left. They must've sorted out their confusion about the 100s and 200s faster than Kyle had thought they would.

Then Pillai did something absolutely amazing. He twirled around in place—while running. He moved his hands over each other and behind his back as he executed a total 360-degree rotation.

Kyle had to slow down a little to nod and give the guy some props.

"Later, dude!" Pillai hollered as he flew past Kyle. He swerved inside to hug the balcony railing that Kyle had wanted to hug.

That's when Kyle remembered that to make the Pacific team, you had to pass the West Coast librarian's final test: a synchronized library-cart drill. The California, Oregon, and Washington State kids weren't pros, but they were definitely the best library-cart handlers in the building.

By the time Kyle completed his circuit around the balcony and reached the 000s door to hand off the cart to Miguel, the Pacific team's second runner, Kathy Narramore from Oregon, was already four doors ahead of him. When she saw a crimp in the carpet, she did a front flip over the rolling buggy so she could pull it behind her for a while before she did a somersaulting backflip so she could push it again.

Meanwhile, Miguel hit the bump and sent a stack of books tumbling off the cart's slanted shelves.

By the time Miguel finally reloaded the cart, pushed it around the balcony, and handed it off to Sierra, the Pacific team's fourth and final runner was ready to lap her.

Sierra made it as far as the 500s door when the Pacific team's closer sprinted across the finish line.

Akimi never even got into the race.

The Hometown Heroes had lost.

The Pacific team took the first medal of the duodecimalthon.

"Congratulations on your Gold medal," said Dr. Zinchenko as she draped a ribboned medallion over each of the winning team members' heads.

"No worries," said Kyle, trying to buck up his teammates, even though he was starting to have those "champions become chumps" feelings again. "We'll take the next one."

"Definitely," said Miguel.

"Unless," said Akimi, "it involves running with a rolling suitcase."

During the lunch break, the Pacific team kids did interviews with NPR, PBS, and the Book Network.

"That used to be us," groused Akimi.

"Come on," said Kyle. "You didn't think we'd win every single game, did you?"

"No. I didn't think it. But I was kind of counting on it anyway."

"My bad," said Miguel. "I lost all that time when I hit that bump."

Kyle glanced at Sierra. She had a smile on her face. Because she was reading again, and apparently, *The Fourteenth Goldfish* by Jennifer L. Holm was a very amusing book.

At two p.m., all eight teams were once again summoned to the second floor.

The library carts, each one still loaded down with three dozen books, were parked, once again, in front of the 000s door.

"Great," muttered Akimi. "A rematch."

"Teams," said Dr. Zinchenko, "it is now time for our second contest. In game number two, you must put all of your books back on the shelves in the exact spot where they belong. Therefore, you will need to first properly determine the full Dewey decimal number for all thirty-six of your assigned books and then place them in their proper shelf slots in your Dewey decimal room."

Kyle looked at Miguel.

"We can do this," said Miguel. "It's why we ran all those drills after school."

"Teams?" said Dr. Zinchenko. "Please return to your carts."

The eight teams clustered around their carts to size up their thirty-six titles.

Miguel, Sierra, and Akimi tilted their heads and squinted. Kyle could tell they were already noodling out numbers.

Great. They could do that part. Kyle would be in charge of running real fast and slamming the books into the shelves.

They had a chance.

A good chance.

It took Team Kyle only one hour and twenty-two minutes to correctly code and reshelf all thirty-six books.

Unfortunately, the Midwest team, led by Marjory Muldauer, did it in under an hour.

Marjory and her teammates would be awarded four Olympian medals.

"Looks like that's one for us"—Marjory smirked at Kyle—"and none for you."

The medal ceremony took place under the Wonder Dome, which, to honor the idea behind the second game, was operating in its spectacular Dewey decimal mode. The ten pizza-slice video screens scrolled constantly changing images associated with each category in the library cataloging system.

"Hey, Kyle," Miguel whispered as Dr. Zinchenko draped an Olympian medal around Marjory Muldauer's neck. "How come they have different names for the medals? Why aren't they all just, you know, 'gold'?"

Kyle shrugged. "Maybe to make it easier for us to remember that we lost *two* different games today."

But tomorrow would be another day.

With two new games to play.

Kyle just hoped his team didn't lose both of those games, too.

20

Charles Chiltington brought a tray of cucumber finger sandwiches (with the crusts trimmed off) into the living room, where his mother was hosting a meeting of the League of Concerned Library Lovers.

The seven ladies and one gentleman in a bow tie were huddled around a laptop, their horrified eyes glued to the screen.

"This is an abomination!" said one of the committee members, watching a recap of the Lemoncello Library Olympics' first day of competition on the Book Network's website.

Charles knew what "abomination" meant (anything greatly disliked). He used big words whenever possible. It impressed teachers, especially when you used words they didn't understand. Charles kept a list: "panacea," "panoply," "pedantic." And those were just the ones that started with "p." He was very sesquipedalian (given to the use of long words) where others were perspicuous (clear in expression and easily understood).

He was also elated (very happy, jubilant, in high spirits) to hear all the adults complaining about Mr. Lemoncello and his egregious (shockingly bad) library.

"It's preposterous," said the gentleman in the bow tie. "Racing around in circles with library carts? Restocking shelves? Are these children applying for part-time jobs? Because they're all far too young to be legally employed."

"Ugh," said Mrs. Tinker. "That Mr. Lemoncello fellow is so incredibly irksome. So is that Russian gal, Dr. Zinfadelski."

"I'm so very confused," said Mrs. Brewster. "Why on earth would a library need a director of holographic imagery?"

"Because it's Disneyland in there!" shouted Mrs. Tinker. "Disneyland, I say!"

"Then we're agreed," said Charles's mother. "Something must be done."

"And may I," said Charles, "as a youth of Alexandriaville, quickly elucidate how fortunate I feel to have you wise and sagacious elders looking out for my best interests as well as the interests of all the young children yet to come?"

Charles knew being smarmy was the best way to get adults to do exactly what you wanted them to do.

"Thank you, Charles," said his mother. "Rose, please

make a note in the official meeting minutes. Resolved: We, the League of Concerned Library Lovers, must, by any means necessary, seize control of Alexandriaville's new public library and wrest it away from that borderline lunatic Luigi Lemoncello."

There was a light rap on the living room door.

"Excuse me," said Chesterton, the butler. "This gentleman insists that he is here for your meeting."

"Are you folks the Concerned Library Lovers?" asked a scrawny old man with a pointy beak who stood timidly in the doorway beside the butler. The man was dressed in a bright blue Windbreaker and was fidgeting with the sweat-stained Toronto Blue Jays baseball cap he held in his hands.

"Do we know you?" asked Charles's mother.

"I don't think so. My name is Peckleman. Woodrow J. Peckleman."

"Of the Geauga County Pecklemans?" twittered Mrs. Tilley.

"No, ma'am. From right here in Alexandriaville. Well, I grew up here, but then I flew the coop."

Charles sniggered. He couldn't help it. Mr. Peckleman looked like a chicken.

"I own the Blue Jay Extended Stay Lodge," said Mr. Peckleman.

"That's Olympia Village," said Charles. "You're Andrew's long-lost great-uncle-twice-removed, correct?"

"That I am."

"Pardon me for asking," said Charles's mother, "but what brings you here, Mr. Pecklestein?"

"It's Peckleman, ma'am. And I won't beat around the bush. I don't like what they're doing inside that Lemoncello Library downtown."

"Neither do we."

"I know. I've seen you folks on TV. Now, like I said, I used to live here in Alexandriaville. Years ago. Grew up with Luigi. Knew him when he was just a little boy, not some kind of fancy billionaire. And let me tell you folks something: Luigi L. Lemoncello was just as irresponsible back then as he is now. Why, in fifth grade, he made up multiplication and division games to make learning math 'more fun.' Pah. Math isn't supposed to be fun. It's math!"

"That's all well and good, Mr. Peckleman, but . . ."

"You people want him out of that library, am I right?"

Charles's mom coyly twiddled her fingertips against her cheek. "Perhaps."

"Well, I know how to do it."

"Really? And what do you require from us in return?"

"Not much. I just need you to talk to that brainy gal from Michigan for me. The tall one on the Midwest team."

"Marjory Muldauer?"

"Yes, ma'am. I've been scoping out all the library lovers bunking at my motel. Looking for just one of 'em to help me do what needs to be done. So far, over a dozen have turned me down. But I have a hunch that Miss Muldauer won't."

"What makes you say that?"

"She's not very fond of all the silly sideshow antics down at Luigi's library. I suspect she wouldn't mind seeing the place run by more responsible adults."

"But, Mr. Peckleman, why do you want *me* to speak with this girl on your behalf?"

"Because, Mrs. Chiltington, she'll listen to someone refined and educated like you. And when *you* offer her a 'Go to College Free' card, I have a feeling Miss Muldauer will become the answer to both our prayers."

21

Team Kyle's bookmobile ride from Olympia Village to the Lemoncello Library was extremely quiet on the second morning of the competition.

Finally, Akimi spoke up. "Wonder what kind of wacky games we can lose today."

"Both of them," said Miguel. "And it'll probably be my fault again, too."

Kyle was also feeling pretty low. But since he was still the team's captain, he decided he needed to give a pep talk. Maybe he could even convince himself that they still had a shot.

"Take it easy, you guys," he said. "Look—if you were playing Mr. Lemoncello's Family Frenzy and the first and second time you rolled the dice, you landed on Sewer Repairs and Dog Pound, would you quit?"

"Yes," said Akimi. "I'd consider it an omen."

"I wouldn't," said Sierra. "Especially since you still have so many more turns to go before anyone wins."

"Exactly," said Kyle. "Well, we've got ten more turns. Right now, the score is Pacific one, Midwest one. All we have to do is win one game and we're tied for first place."

Miguel stroked his chin. "Hmm. When you put it like that . . ."

"We're still currently tied for last place," said Akimi.

"So is everybody else," said Kyle as the bookmobile pulled up to the front of the library. "So let's go in there and change that!"

"Fine," said Akimi, who was pretty immune to pep talks. "Whatever."

The setup in the Rotunda Reading Room was slightly different for the second day of the competition.

The two circles of desks closest to the center of the room had been roped off to the crowd of spectators, many of whom were now upstairs on the second and third floors with the news cameras, peering down at the action from the upper decks.

Kyle noticed that Mr. Peckleman, the motel owner, was in the crowd clustered at the remaining tables on the first floor. He was staring up at the Wonder Dome in awe.

"Ah, the sandhill crane migration!" Kyle heard him exclaim to nobody in particular. "Isn't it marvelous?"

The entire underbelly of the Wonder Dome had been

transformed into a fluttering flock of birds, soaring across an unbelievably blue sky, swooping through a clay-colored desert landscape.

"Welcome, bookworms!"

Kyle looked up.

Mr. Lemoncello had just climbed on top of the balcony railing outside his private suite—on the third floor! He was wearing a leather aviator helmet with goggles and had a pair of feathered wings strapped to his back.

"Today," announced Mr. Lemoncello, "in our third and fourth games, you will use the library to help your imagination take flight, much as I am about to do."

"No!" screamed Mrs. Lonni Gause, the frazzled holographic librarian, who popped into view behind the circulation desk. "Don't jump! You'll end up a heap of crumpled bones, just like the old library ended up a heap of crushed rubble! And they'll be back! The book haters with their bulldozers! They always come back! I hear them rumbling up Main Street now!"

"Fear not, Mrs. Gause," cried Mr. Lemoncello. "If anyone should ever again threaten this library, I will fly to its aid, much as I should've flown to it all those years ago. But alas, I was too busy doing business in Beijing to come home and save my beloved library, leaving you to ask, 'Where's Waldo?' even though my first name was, and still is, Luigi. Moving on. I'd like to quote the lyrics of Rodgers and Hammerstein—something that's extremely easy to do when you're in a library near 782.14 and all those magnificent Broadway show tunes—'I flit, I float, I fleetly flee, I fly!' "

Mr. Lemoncello leapt off the railing.

Two thousand spectators gasped. Several hid their eyes.

Too bad. They missed the whole thing.

Mr. Lemoncello floated in a graceful arc, then soared up to join the migrating Canadian geese now flocking in a V formation on the Wonder Dome video screens.

After leading the geese toward Montreal, Mr. Lemoncello drifted down to buzz and salute the statues perched atop the pillars at the base of the dome. The holographic heroes were different again. Kyle turned around so he could read all their names: Amelia Earhart, Charles Lindbergh, Neil Armstrong, Bessie Coleman, Jimmy Doolittle, Howard Hughes, Sally Ride, Billy Mitchell, the Tuskegee Airmen, and some kind of monk whose pedestal was labeled "Eilmer of Malmesbury."

"They're all famous aviators," said Miguel as Mr. Lemoncello executed a tucked-knee roll and soared around the rotunda like Peter Pan.

Actually, he flew *exactly* like the star of a touring production of *Peter Pan* that Kyle had seen at the civic center.

Because now, in the shafts of sunlight streaming through the arched windows at the base of the dome, Kyle could see cables hooked to a harness under Mr. Lemoncello's wings.

As he spread out his arms and fluttered toward the floor, the audience applauded wildly.

"Thank you, thank you," said Mr. Lemoncello when his feet finally touched down.

He slipped out of his flying harness, and his wings shot back up toward the ceiling.

"Yowza! That's almost as much fun as the hover ladders. Almost. Teams, your first challenge today is to make your ideas take flight, something that's very easy to do inside a library."

"So long as nobody bulldozes it down!" cried Mrs. Gause, whose flickering image was still being projected behind the circulation desk.

"Yes. Thank you for that, Lonni." Mr. Lemoncello pushed up his goggles. "Dr. Zinchenko? Will you kindly take over? I must go assemble our esteemed panel of judges."

"Of course." Dr. Z popped up behind the center desk like a hand puppet. Mrs. Gause disappeared.

"Amaze me!" cried Mr. Lemoncello as he dashed toward the towering fiction bookshelves and disappeared through another secret door that whooshed sideways in the shelves.

"Teams," said Dr. Zinchenko, "on each of your worktables, you will find a sheet of eight-and-a-half-by-eleven paper, one standard paper clip, three inches of tape, one plastic bag containing a dollop of glue, and a stapler loaded with three staples."

Kyle and his teammates checked out their reading desk. Everything on Dr. Z's supply list was arranged in a tidy row.

"To win today's first competition, you must design the paper airplane that stays aloft the longest. In the case of a tie, our esteemed panel of judges will also award points for style and what aviators call derring-do."

At the Midwest team's desk, Marjory Muldauer shot her hand into the air and waved it around annoyingly.

"Yes? Is there a question?"

"Just one," said Marjory, folding her arms across her chest. "What does building a paper airplane have to do with the study of library science?"

"Simple," said Dr. Zinchenko. "The flight test will take place in three hours, at precisely one o'clock. You may use the intervening time and the library's vast resources to do research before building your planes. Or not. The choice, as always, is yours."

22

The 700s room on the second floor (named for the Dewey decimal designation for the arts) was crowded with Library Olympians.

Every team had raced up the steps, hoping to be the first to grab *The Paper Airplane Book* by Seymour Simon. Its call number was 745.592.

Fortunately, the Lemoncello Library had eight copies of the book on its shelves.

"You guys?" whispered Miguel after the team had grabbed their copy of the book and huddled together under a Nerf basketball hoop in a secluded nook so they could talk without all the other teams overhearing what they were saying. "Everybody's reading this same book."

"Because there are all sorts of neat paper airplane designs in here," said Sierra.

"But," said Kyle, "if we follow one of these sketches, our plane will end up being just like everybody else's."

"We need my dad," said Akimi.

"Huh?" said Miguel.

"Well, not my dad, exactly. But someone with his architect-slash-engineer brain."

Miguel slapped his forehead with his palm. He had an idea.

"Aerospace engineering," he whispered.

"Six hundred and twenty-nine point one," added Sierra.

It was Akimi's turn to say, "Huh?"

"Sorry. That's the Dewey decimal number for aviation engineering."

"Oh. Right. I knew that."

"It's next door," said Kyle, checking out the other teams. All seven of them had settled in at collaboration stations to pore through the paper airplane book. "Follow my lead, guys."

He loudly closed their copy of the paper airplane book. "Okay, team. I think that'll work. Come on. Let's go fold some paper and use our paper clip."

"And the glue," said Akimi. "Don't forget, we have a whole dollop of glue."

The four teammates sauntered out of the 700s room. Miguel whistled casually. Sierra hummed along.

The other teams were too busy debating the design of their paper airplanes to pay them much attention.

When Kyle, Akimi, Miguel, and Sierra slipped next door to the 600s room, the place was empty. Since the 600s were all about technology and applied sciences, the team passed several animated exhibits and dioramas depicting inventions and one about industrial gases, which used Mr. Lemoncello's patented smell-a-vision technology and reeked of rotten eggs.

"Great," muttered Akimi. "We had to come in here on sulfur day."

When they turned the corner at the end of a bookshelf labeled "629–632," they saw a holographic image of a bald man with a paintbrush mustache projected behind a desk. He wore a three-piece wool suit and fiddled with a small rocket.

"That looks like Robert Goddard," said Akimi. "My dad told me about him. Goddard invented the first liquid-fueled rocket."

"He's also on an old airmail stamp," said Miguel.

The others gave him quizzical looks.

"Stamp collecting is a very interesting hobby."

"Robert Goddard really was a rocket scientist," said Akimi. "Maybe he can help us design a better paper airplane."

The teammates moved closer to the hologram's very real metal desk.

"Hello," the hologram said, "my name is Robert. You can call me Bob. I designed and built airplanes and space-ships. When I was your age, I was considered a nerd. Now I'm on an airmail stamp."

"See?" said Miguel. "Told you."

"Professor Goddard," said Akimi, "what's the best design for our paper airplane?"

"That depends on your objective. Are you going for distance or aeronautical acrobatics?"

"Distance, sir," said Akimi. "Whoever can keep their paper plane aloft the longest wins."

"Then you should be folding what we rocket scientists call a glider."

"Because it glides?" asked Kyle.

"Precisely. I suggest going with a Seagull. Remember to line up the wing flaps for good balance. Set the dihedral angle flat or slightly up, the vertical stabilizers to approximately forty-five degrees to the plane of the wings . . ."

"The plane has a plane?" Kyle was totally lost.

"Keep going," said Akimi, who apparently understood engineer mumbo jumbo.

"Do not use the elevators or your craft will stall."

"No worries," said Miguel. "We always use the spiral staircases."

Akimi and Goddard stared at him.

"Never mind these guys," said Akimi. "I understand what you mean. My dad designed the library's front doors."

"Incorporating the old bank's vault door?"

"Yep."

"I am impressed," said Bob. "Will you be the one launching the craft?"

"Yes," said Kyle, Miguel, and Sierra.

"Excellent. Use a soft or medium throw by gripping the underside of the nose. This aircraft flies best when launched level or at a slight up angle from a high place. A detailed schematic with complete instructions is available in the top drawer of my desk. Good luck. And happy paper-folding!"

Robert Goddard vanished.

Kyle pulled open the desk drawer.

There were eight copies of the Seagull paper airplane design.

"I guess there's one for every team," he said.

"If they think to come in here," said Miguel.

But none of them did.

They were too busy, back at their worktables down in the Rotunda Reading Room, folding the paper airplanes they had chosen from that one book in the 700s room.

At one p.m., the eight teams brought their finished aircraft up to the third floor.

The eight designated fliers stepped up to the balcony railing, where they were joined by Dr. Zinchenko and the panel of holographic judges: Orville and Wilbur Wright, Amelia Earhart, Neil Armstrong, and Leonardo da Vinci.

The spectators were ringed around the rotunda, eagerly anticipating the paper aircraft taking flight.

Leonardo, decked out in his flowing robes and floppy Renaissance cap, gave the prelaunch countdown: "*Cinque, quattro, tre, due, uno*—blast off!"

Eight paper airplanes took off. The crowd cheered, rooting for their favorite fliers.

"That's one small toss for a sheet of paper," said Neil Armstrong, "one giant heave for paperkind."

Most of the paper airplanes drifted in looping circles, spiraling down the three stories under the dome in one or two minutes.

Akimi's carefully constructed Seagull, however, stayed aloft for four whole minutes. The audience gasped in astonishment as it glided along, scarcely losing altitude. Finally, after what seemed like forever, it gently drifted to the floor, where it made a soft landing.

"Woo-hoo!" shouted Kyle.

He looked down and saw Akimi's father in the audience on the first floor. Akimi's dad marched over to the winning glider, proudly plucked it off the floor, and gave his daughter a thumbs-up!

"Thanks, Dad!" Akimi shouted.

Orville and Wilbur Wright announced that the hometown team's glider had just set a new "hand-folded paper plane" indoor flight-time record.

"And it didn't get lost," added Amelia Earhart.

Akimi accepted the team's Top Gun medal from Dr. Zinchenko.

And just like that, the Hometown Heroes were tied for first place.

23

"And now," announced Dr. Zinchenko, "it is time for today's second game. This way, please."

The teams followed her from the third-floor railing to the nearby Electronic Learning Center. All the video games and flight simulators were dark. The arcade was eerily quiet. Kyle noticed something new in what had always been his favorite room in the library: One whole wall was covered, floor to ceiling, with a panoramic (but blank) video screen. As Kyle squinted at the wide swath of shiny white, he noticed a series of evenly spaced glowing green LEDs at eye level on the wall.

Kyle couldn't move closer to examine the screen, because the area fifteen feet in front of it had been fenced off with a series of brass poles and velvet ropes.

Suddenly, the floor on the other side of the ropes opened. Up came the smiling head and extremely long neck of a life-size *Apatosaurus*—what everybody used to call a *Brontosaurus,* thanks to *The Flintstones.*

The giant dinosaur had leaves stuck between its teeth. Its breath reeked of rancid salad, smelling worse than the middle school cafeteria that time all the refrigerators stopped working on Taco Tuesday.

"Woo-weee!" cried Mr. Lemoncello, who, in a complete cowboy costume, was riding in a saddle strapped around the giant audio-animatronic *Apatosaurus*'s neck. "I knew the dinosaurs were extinct, but I didn't know they were extra stinky, too." He took in a deep breath. "Ah, isn't smell-a-vision wondermous?"

He unbuckled some sort of seat belt and hopped out of his saddle.

"Thank you, Brontie," he said to the big *Apatosaurus.* "By the way, I love your sister Charlotte. Now, please—go floss."

The enormous creature roared pleasantly, rattling all the blank video screens in the game room, then disappeared back into the floor, which closed up around it like a collapsing ring of tiles.

"Since today is all about flights of fancy and fancy flights, our next contest is to see which of you would make the paleontologically perfect prehistoric pterodactyl."

Mr. Lemoncello flung open his arms toward the wide screen filling the back wall.

"This room was recently equipped with my Imagination Factory's brand-new, revolutionary Gesticulatron

Gameware. Motion sensors in that hugerific video wall can read a gamer's body language and use human gestures to control the actions of your avatar inside the video game. Yes, with the Lemoncello Gesticulatron Motion Detector, you can fly through the sky like Harriet the Spy, if Harriet the Spy could fly."

Marjory Muldauer sighed very audibly and, once again, shot her arm into the air.

"I see from my own internal gesticulation sensors that we have a question," said Mr. Lemoncello. "Either that or Ms. Muldauer is attempting to hail a taxi indoors."

All the other kids (including Marjory's teammates) chuckled.

Marjory ignored them.

"Yes, Ms. Muldauer?" said Mr. Lemoncello.

"What does flying like a dinosaur have to do with libraries?"

"Actually," said Mr. Lemoncello, "pterodactyls were not dinosaurs but rather flying reptiles that existed from the Late Triassic through the Jurassic and most of the Cretaceous eras. They missed, however, the disco era, for which they were extremely grateful. All of this information I first learned, years ago, at my local library. Now we can learn even more by bringing these extinct creatures back to virtual yet historically accurate life. This is how the library of the future can present the facts of the past. Dr. Zinchenko? Kindly explain how this next game will be played." He tugged at his fringed leggings. "I'll be monitoring this fourth contest from my private suite down the hall. I need to change out of my chaps before I chafe."

Spurs jingling, Mr. Lemoncello moseyed out of the Electronic Learning Center.

"For our next competition," announced Dr. Zinchenko, "each team will choose one player who will report back here in two hours. Your chosen flier will, with arm gestures and body movements, control the flight of a single pterodactyl. The player to reach the finish line of our airborne obstacle course first will be today's second medalist. Launch time is four p.m. Until then, all of the library's vast resources are available to you. Including, of course, all the games here in the Electronic Learning Center."

The blackened video screens on all the game consoles filling the room sprang to life. Dings, pings, bells, whoops, and techno music filled the air.

"Awesome," said a kid from the Southeast team when the Mars rover simulator whirred awake. "Who wants to race around the rings of Saturn with me?"

Kyle was tempted.

In fact, he was practically drooling.

Then Akimi tapped him on the shoulder.

"You're flying our pterodactyl, correct?"

"Sure. If you guys think I should."

"Yo," said Miguel. "It's a video game. You're our gamer."

"The only flying I've ever done," said Sierra, "was with

Max, Fang, Iggy, and Nudge in James Patterson's Maximum Ride books."

Kyle stared at all the kids blasting through outer space, flinging catapults of fire at castle walls, or scuba diving with dolphins on the glowing game screens surrounding him.

"So," he said, sighing, "where do I learn about dinosaurs?"

"The five hundreds room," his three teammates said in unison (because they'd all paid attention during those after-school Dewey decimal drills).

"It's downstairs," said Akimi. "Right below us. You can't miss it. There's a big *Apatosaurus* named Brontie inside."

With his teammates' help, Kyle found several books about flying creatures from the prehistoric era.

Pterodactyls had wings formed by a thin skin and muscle membrane stretching from one of their elongated fingers to their hind limbs. They looked like four-legged, pointy-nosed kites.

"They ate meat and fish," said Miguel. "Guess they wouldn't go for that birdseed Andrew's always pouring into Mr. Peckleman's bird feeders back at the motel."

"Why does that crazy old guy like birds so much?" said Akimi, flipping through a dinosaur picture book. "There are gobs of white bird poop splatted all over the cars in the motel parking lot."

"He's a birdbrain," said Miguel. "Get it? Bird-brain?"

"Yeah," said Akimi. "I got it."

"Have you ever played one of these motion-sensor games?" Sierra asked Kyle.

"Once. My cousin has a Kinect on his Xbox 360. We played a game where you karate kick and shoot lightning bolts at each other."

"Cool," said Miguel.

"Totally. But I'm guessing Mr. Lemoncello's Gesticula-tron technology is way more sophisticated."

Kyle's team wasn't the only group in the 500s room doing dinosaur research. Several other teams had had the same idea. Just about every book about pterosaurs (from the Greek words for "wing" and "lizard") was flying off the shelves.

When it was nearly four o'clock, a slender boy in blue jeans from the Southwest team sauntered over to Kyle, Akimi, Sierra, and Miguel, who were slumped in beanbag chairs resembling dinosaur eggs.

"Excellent display of aviation engineering," he said. "Your glider design was flawless."

"Thanks. I'm Akimi Hughes." She shot out her hand. "I was chief engineer on the paper airplane project."

"I'm Angus Harper. From Texas."

"My dad's an engineer," said Akimi, sounding sort of self-satisfied. "Guess I'm just hardwired to design stuff."

Harper nodded. "My dad's a test pilot. He's been givin' me flyin' lessons since I was six."

"You're kidding," said Kyle, closing his dinosaur book.

"Nope. I've already been offered an appointment to the United States Air Force Academy."

"Even though you're still in middle school?" said Sierra.

"Well, I guess some of us are just 'hardwired' to be flyboys."

"So," said Miguel, clearing his throat, "who's going to fly the pterodactyl for your team?"

"I reckon I might give it a whirl. See you folks upstairs."

Angus Harper ambled away.

"So," Kyle said to Sierra, "tell me about those kids in Maximum Ride. How exactly did *they* fly?"

"Genetic mutation," said Sierra.

"Oh. Guess we don't really have time for that. . . ."

"Don't worry, bro," Miguel told Kyle. "If the Texas Tornado takes the next medal, we'll still be tied for first place."

"Yeah," said Akimi. "With three other teams."

At exactly four p.m., Kyle stood on a pair of glowing green footprints in a line with seven other contestants facing the blank video wall.

Television cameras were set up in the Electronic Learning Center so spectators, in the library and at home, could watch the great flying reptile race. The illuminated floor markers put six feet of space between each player. That way, they'd have plenty of room to flap and flail their arms.

Angus Harper was on Kyle's right.

A girl from the Northeast team, wearing a hijab, was on his left.

She was staring at Kyle.

"Um, hi," he said. "I'm Kyle."

"Yes. I am aware of this fact."

"So, uh, what's your name?"

"Abia Sulayman. And you will soon be eating my exhaust fumes."

Kyle nodded. "Good to know."

Dr. Zinchenko paced in front of the players, her hands clasped firmly behind her back.

"The motion sensors in the screen will detect your arm, head, and torso movement," she explained. "Do not step off your footprint markers at any time during today's race. If you do, you will lose control of your flying reptile and it will crash. If you wish to go left, lean that way. To go right, lean right. Raise your head to gain elevation; look down at the floor to dive or swoop. When you flap your arms, your pterodactyl will flap its wings. Any questions?"

"Yes, ma'am," said Angus. "How do we gun our bird? I feel the need—the need for speed."

"To accelerate, simply flap your arms faster. However, be advised: The faster you fly, the more energy your pterodactyl will consume. Your winged avatar will have a 'life battery' icon glowing on its back. If you burn through your fuel, you will also crash. The object of this game is to be the first to safely reach the volcano crater on the island at the far side of the sea."

As Dr. Zinchenko spoke, the wall behind her turned into a spectacular prehistoric world. Kyle could see dinosaurs munching on tall tree branches far off in the rain forest. Then a *Tyrannosaurus rex* roared and stomped through the leafy jungle, causing a leaping herd of *Velociraptors* to screech and flee. It was like being inside that movie *Jurassic Park*. All the creatures Kyle had read about and studied in the dinosaur books downstairs were now swarming across the giant video screen in front of him.

"Give me eight pterodactyls," Dr. Zinchenko called out. Instantly, eight winged creatures appeared on the screen, one stationed in front of each player.

"Flap your arms," instructed Dr. Zinchenko.

The eight players did. The flying reptiles beat their wings up and down in sync with their human counterparts.

Suddenly, a massive image of Mr. Lemoncello's face appeared on the video wall.

"Release the kraken!" he cried.

And the pterodactyl race was on.

Kyle flapped his arms and raised his chin.

His flying reptile soared toward the sky.

The game was responding like his cousin's Xbox, only Mr. Lemoncello's body-motion sensors were, as Kyle had suspected they might be, much more sophisticated and sensitive.

He tilted his body sideways and his dino-bird sliced through the narrow opening in a vine-tangled clump of prehistoric trees.

After clearing that obstacle, Kyle quickly ducked left to escape the gaping jaws of a lunging *Tyrannosaurus rex*. Eight of those screeching, short-armed monsters had appeared to snap at the eight flying pterodactyls.

Three of Kyle's competitors went down, including the kid from Marjory Muldauer's team.

Angus Harper and Abia Sulayman were just off Kyle's wings. He cleared the *T. rex* trap and reached a sandy beach where some smaller dinosaurs were building nests. Kyle waved his arms and soared across the choppy sea.

On the distant horizon, Kyle could see a volcano spewing molten lava. The finish line.

He flapped his arms faster.

When he did, the battery icon on the back of his pterodactyl dipped down to three-quarters. Dr. Zinchenko had been right. Flying fast drained your dino-bird's life force even faster.

Suddenly, another "flying reptile" from the dinosaur books appeared in the sky: a giant *Pteranodon* with a thirty-foot wingspan. It was four times as wide as the other fliers and shrieked at the runts in the pterodactyl pack.

Kyle kept his cool and aimed his reptile into what he hoped would be the *Pteranodon*'s blind spot. The bigger beast gobbled down one flier, which freaked out Stephanie Youngerman from the Mountain team. She shrieked, jumped off her floor mark, and crashed into the ocean.

Only Kyle, Angus, and Abia were left in the race.

"If I was flying any faster," Angus shouted, "I'd catch up with tomorrow!"

"Where you would meet me!" cried the girl.

The two kids flailed their arms furiously. Both of their avatars shot off like rocket ships, streaking the cloudless sky with white contrails.

Kyle could see Abia tuck in her arms and shoulders, making her profile sleekly aerodynamic. She inched ahead of Angus.

Kyle tried his best to mimic Abia's moves but was buffeted in the wake created by her back draft. He moved his arms up and down and up and down until he looked like a berserk bicycle pump.

He whooshed forward faster but his battery icon dipped down to one-quarter. Its green light was on its way to red.

And the volcanic island was still miles away.

No way would Kyle make it without running out of juice.

He pulled back on his speed, wishing this flying pterodactyl game came with power pellets of some kind. In most video games, there was some way to restore life force after you'd been weakened, and play on. But in this game, there was nothing except the two other pterodactyls, the ocean, and the distant volcano.

Then Kyle remembered something from his library research.

The pterodactyl was a carnivore.

It ate meat and fish.

Maybe there were some virtual fish in the virtual ocean below.

It was worth a shot.

He lowered his chin and sent his dino-bird swooping into a dive, then leveled it out when it was just a few inches above the video ocean's churning waves.

The water was swarming with fish.

Kyle opened his mouth.

The pterodactyl opened its long spiky jaws.

Kyle did a goosenecked head bob.

The pterodactyl bobbed and scooped up a mouthful of fish.

Kyle heard a WHIRR-DING! sound effect as his red battery icon glowed green and grew from nearly empty to completely full. Raising his head, Kyle gained altitude and zipped across the sky.

He leveled off and aimed for the volcano. Abia Sulayman, who was maybe three hundred feet ahead of him, stalled in midair. Her battery icon was solid red. Kyle shot past her. She dropped like a chunk of fossilized dinosaur bone.

Ahead, Angus Harper appeared to be flying on vapors—barely sputtering, lurching and jerking forward.

His battery icon went red just as Kyle zipped past him.

"You must've cheated!" Harper screamed right before his pterodactyl plummeted to its watery grave.

"Nope!" shouted Kyle, executing a pretty nifty barrel roll by swiveling his hips. "I just did my homework!"

When Kyle's pterodactyl reached the volcano, a hot-air balloon rose from the smoldering basin. In the balloon's wicker gondola was a video-game image of Mr. Lemoncello dressed like the Wizard of Oz.

"Hearty and splendiferous congratulations, Kyle Keeley," boomed Mr. Lemoncello. "You played hard but you studied harder. You are the true Lord of the Fliers. Therefore, by the power vested in me by the electric company, even though they didn't know I would be wearing a vest today, I hereby award you the Olympian Researcher medal for meritorious fish mongering. Tonight, at Olympia Village, in honor of your cleverosity, you and your teammates shall feast upon fish sticks and Filet-O-Fish sandwiches."

Kyle hoped there might be some kind of cake for dinner, too, because he and his teammates definitely had something to celebrate.

All of a sudden, they were in the lead!

26

Marjory Muldauer watched as the triumphant Kyle Keeley and his happy crew of crumbums climbed into their bookmobile.

All four were merrily flapping their arms, giving each other high and low fives.

Marjory still couldn't believe what she had just witnessed. Kids waving their arms up and down to make fake video creatures fly to a phony volcano?

Shame on you, Mr. Lemoncello, she thought, seething. *If I didn't need a scholarship to even think about attending college, I'd quit these inane games!*

Marjory and her teammates climbed into their bookmobile for the ride back to Olympia Village, which, in her opinion, was really just a cheesy, mid-level extended stay motel—the kind of place typically frequented by sketchy traveling salespeople and high school athletics teams.

Marjory grabbed a book off a shelf in the back. *Bleak House* by Charles Dickens. It matched her mood.

"Shake it off, you guys," coached Margaret Miles, the librarian who was one of the Midwest team's chaperones. "So what if the Ohio kids won two medals today? There are eight more games left to play. This thing is far from over."

"That Kyle Keeley kid is good," said Nicole Wisniewski, one of Marjory's wimpy teammates. "He was smart, the way he recharged his pterodactyl's battery."

"He's a gamer," Marjory snapped at Nicole. "Of course he won the video game. But he doesn't know diddly about the Dewey decimal system. That's why I beat him in the book reshelving game."

"Actually," said Nicole, "we all beat him."

Marjory blew her teammate a wet raspberry. "Yeah. Right. Like you guys would've had a chance without me."

"Marjory?" said Ms. Miles. "Remember, there is no 'I' in 'team.'"

So? thought Marjory. *Because there is definitely an "m" and an "e" for me!*

To chill out after such a lousy day, Marjory headed into the motel lobby and started reorganizing the rack of tourist brochures.

All the other Library Olympians, including Marjory's worthless teammates, were at the pizza place next door to the motel, having dinner and probably playing more mind-numbing video games.

128

Andrew Peckleman, the boy with the Olympic-sized goggle glasses who worked at the motel, came into the lobby when she was about halfway done.

"Are you going with an alphabetical classification system or something a bit more complex?"

"I'm categorizing them according to attraction type," said Marjory. "Outdoor activities, historical sites, shopping opportunities—subcategorized, of course, into fashion, antiques, and souvenirs."

"Of course," said Andrew.

"And, over here, you'll find dining options."

Andrew smiled. "Isn't informational organization awesome?"

"Yes," said Marjory. "It's certainly more intellectually stimulating than video games."

"Rough day at the Library Olympics?"

"Ha! That Lemoncello Library is as ridiculous and absurd as Mr. Lemoncello himself."

"True," said Andrew through his nose. "I'm afraid Mr. Lemoncello doesn't like libraries qua libraries."

Marjory nearly gasped. "You use the word 'qua'?"

"Yes," said Andrew, finger-sliding his glasses up the bridge of his nose. "But only when its usage is appropriate."

A lady wearing a fur-fringed jacket floated into the lobby.

"Hello, Andrew."

"Oh, hello, Mrs. Chiltington. What're you doing here?"

"I came to see Miss Muldauer."

"Who are you?" asked Marjory. "And why do you have a dead animal wrapped around your neck?"

"There's a slight nip in the air, dear. Andrew, would you kindly excuse us? I need to talk to Miss Muldauer in private."

"But . . ."

"Andrew?" his uncle Woody called from outside the front doors. "We need to go grease the baffles on the bird feeders."

"Right now?"

"The sooner, the better. I noticed a squirrel having an upside-down feast on feeder number eight. We need to put an end to that. A slicker surface might do the trick."

"But . . ."

"Say goodbye to Marjory, Andrew," suggested Mrs. Chiltington.

"Okay. See you later, Marjory. I have to go to work."

Mrs. Chiltington waited for him and his uncle to walk down the driveway.

Then she pounced.

"Miss Muldauer, may I be frank with you?"

Marjory shrugged. "I don't care."

"I came here this evening as a representative of the League of Concerned Library Lovers."

"Who are they?"

"A group of local citizens who love libraries and

consider Mr. Luigi L. Lemoncello to be a threat to all that we hold dear."

"The man is a major-league wackaloon," said Marjory.

"That he is." Mrs. Chiltington glanced around to make absolutely certain they were alone in the lobby. "I was wondering if you might be able to help Mr. Peckleman and I with a small . . . *project*?"

"I'm kind of busy trying to win these games."

"This won't take much of your time. I promise. But if we work together, I feel confident, we will both be quite satisfied with the end result."

"What do you mean?"

"With your assistance, Marjory, I firmly believe we will convince Mr. Lemoncello to abandon his infantile and dangerously contagious ideas about how a library should be run. Certain things don't belong in our temples of knowledge. Things like flying dinosaur video games."

"So why do you need me?"

"Because the books in the Lemoncello Library are currently off-limits to everyone except you thirty-two Olympians."

"What?" said Marjory, arching an eyebrow. "You want me to check out a book?"

"That's right, Marjory. A book. Just one."

"We can't. Not during the games."

"You strike me as a clever young lady. Surely you can find a way to skirt the rules?"

"But what about my scholarship?"

"Do this for me, and you won't need Mr. Lemoncello's money. Mr. Peckleman and I will personally guarantee funding for your college education. Call it a 'Go to College Free' card. My family is extremely wealthy, Marjory. Has been for centuries."

Interesting. By removing one book from the stacks, Marjory could help these locals put an end to Mr. Lemoncello's misguided notions about how a library should be run and, at the same time, earn herself a full-ride college scholarship.

"So, what makes this one book so special?"

"It is, as they say, the straw that will break the camel's back. Once it leaves the Alexandriaville Public Library, we feel quite confident that Mr. Luigi Lemoncello will want to leave, too."

27

Kyle wasn't worried when Dr. Zinchenko made her morning announcements at Olympia Village on day three of the games.

"Today's two competitions will both be centered on books."

Kyle knew Sierra Russell could handle anything bookish the game makers threw at her.

"Today's your day to shine," he told her.

"I'll do my best," said Sierra.

When the bookmobiles arrived at the Lemoncello Library, the security guards, Clarence and Clement, gave each team member a brand-new smartphone.

"You will need it for today's first game," said Clarence.

"But you get to keep it, too," added Clement.

Sweet, thought Kyle. Even if his team lost this round, they'd all just scored some excellent swag.

The eight teams were assigned work desks in the rotunda. Spectators crowded around the edge of the circular room.

"Please access the Web browser on your phones," said Dr. Zinchenko from her position behind the central desk, "and go to Lemoncello.it."

Kyle did. Then he helped Sierra do it, too. Miguel and Akimi were fine on their own.

"Please enter game code one-zero-zero-two-four."

All the players did.

"Excellent," said Dr. Zinchenko.

Overhead, the Wonder Dome turned into a giant game screen reading "Welcome to the Battle of the Books."

"Please enter your first and last names and, when you have done so, tap 'Join Game.' When you are all online, I, as the quizmaster, will show you a series of ten questions, each one with four possible answers. For each question, you will have ten seconds to make your selection on your phone screen. Lemoncello.it will instantaneously calculate your score based on correctness and speed of answering. It will then post a leaderboard for the top five players. In the event of a tie, the team with the most players in the top five will be awarded today's first medal, the Libris."

Up on the Wonder Dome, thirty-two brightly colored names in a balloon font popped into view as the players finished tapping them into their phones.

"Let us begin," said Dr. Zinchenko. "First question: In which book does a character bounce a pinecone off someone's head?"

Tense, clock-ticking music throbbed out of the Rotunda Reading Room's hidden speakers.

Four answers were displayed on the dome, each identified with a geometric shape. A square for *Ungifted* by Gordon Korman, a triangle for *A Tangle of Knots* by Lisa Graff, a hexagon for *Twerp* by Mark Goldblatt, and an oval for *The Postcard* by Tony Abbott.

"The square," whispered Sierra.

Kyle, Akimi, and Miguel didn't waste any time second-guessing her answer, because the countdown clock had already slid from ten seconds to five by the time they'd finished reading all the possible answers.

A gong sounded when the timer hit zero. The red square for *Ungifted* lit up and was given a check mark as the correct answer. According to the scoreboard on the ceiling, thirty of the thirty-two players had answered correctly, including, of course, all four players from Ohio.

"Way to go, Sierra!" said Kyle.

"Question two," said Dr. Zinchenko. "The Watson family went to Birmingham, Alabama, in 1963. In what city did the Watson family actually live?"

Four choices filled all the phone screens: Detroit, Kansas City, Kalamazoo, and Flint.

"Flint," said Sierra.

All the players on the hometown team tapped the oval icon for Flint.

Sierra's answer, once again, was correct.

"Boo-yah," said Kyle.

Suddenly, Marjory Muldauer, two desks away, leapt up from her seat.

"Dr. Zinchenko?"

"Yes, Ms. Muldauer?"

She pointed at Sierra. "That girl from Ohio is telling her teammates what answer to give."

Trembling slightly, Sierra stood up, too. "Is that against the rules, Dr. Zinchenko?"

Kyle stood up beside her. "Because you didn't say we couldn't help each other."

"Yeah," said Miguel, standing up, too.

"What they said," added Akimi as she stood to join her teammates.

"You are correct," said Dr. Zinchenko. "I did not specifically state that collaboration would be prohibited."

"But it's cheating!" hollered Marjory. She whirled around and glared at Kyle. "This isn't flap-your-arms-and-do-the-chicken-dance, Kyle Keeley. This is serious. 'Battle of the Books' serious. Everybody on your team needs to know the material, inside and out."

"I agree with Miss Muldauer," boomed Mr. Lemoncello. His huge face, looking weirdly warped around the edges, was now filling all the video screens under the dome. "As much as I love teamwork, for this game, you all need to fly solo, like Han in Star Wars, although he always had Chewbacca in the copilot seat. But that is neither here nor there, because it is in a galaxy far, far away. Play on, Olympians. And henceforth, there shall be no consultation amongst teammates. Kindly keep your eyes on your own phone."

The Battle of the Books continued.

Kyle got a couple of answers right on his own, but he took longer to respond than everybody else, so his name never appeared on the leaderboard again. After the ninth question was answered, Marjory Muldauer, Sierra Russell, and a girl from Knoxville, Tennessee, named Jennifer Greene were all tied for first place.

"Here is your final question," said Dr. Zinchenko. "Once again, you will have ten seconds to choose your answer. In which book is a toddler worshipped by cockroaches?"

Wow! Kyle actually knew that one, because the past summer he'd read the book. He quickly tapped the purple hexagon for *Gregor the Overlander* by Suzanne Collins, who had also written *The Hunger Games*.

The gong sounded.

Kyle's answer was correct.

Sierra's, however, wasn't.

"I'm sorry," she said. "I read that book when I was six. I forgot. . . ."

"It's okay," said Kyle.

Meanwhile, at the Midwest team's table, people were jumping up and doing bad potato-masher dances.

Jennifer Greene from the Southeastern team must've chosen the wrong answer, too. Because according to the leaderboard, Marjory Muldauer had just won the games' fifth medal.

28

"We're still tied for first place," Kyle reminded Sierra.

Sierra lowered her eyes. "But I let you guys down."

"Not really," said Akimi. "Did you see any of us winning that last game? I thought the cockroach book was *Harry Potter and the Prisoner of Azkaban,* because they eat Cockroach Clusters at Honeydukes."

"We'll win the next medal," said Miguel. "You'll see."

"Moving on to game six," said Dr. Zinchenko, still stationed behind the circular librarian's desk at the center of the room. "Please focus your eyes on the area between the lobby archway and the entrance to the Children's Room."

Clarence and Clement came into the rotunda to clear a path. Spectators gladly moved out of their way. The musclemen were both pretty ginormous.

"Players?" said Dr. Zinchenko. "This will be another

solo competition. Please pick one player to represent your team. A parade of costumed characters as well as stagehands carrying props will soon march from the lobby, promenade along the back wall, and exit into the Children's Room. Your chosen player will assemble the characters and props into titles of famous children's books. The player who can correctly figure out the titles and identify their authors the fastest will win our sixth medal, the 'I Did It!'"

"I played a mix-and-match game like this once in a magazine," said Miguel.

"Good," said Sierra. "You should be our player for this round."

"No way. You fall off a horse, what do you do?"

"Bruise your butt?" said Akimi.

"No," said Kyle with a laugh. "You climb right back into the saddle."

Miguel agreed. "This is your saddle, Sierra."

"I don't want to lose another game. . . ."

"You won't," said Kyle. "You're our number one bookworm. In a good way."

"Not in the icky insect-that-bores-through-paper way," added Akimi.

"Thanks," said Sierra. "I think."

"Let the title parade begin!" commanded Dr. Zinchenko.

A recorded brass band struck up a Sousa march as a bizarre assortment of costumed characters and prop carriers strolled out of the lobby, around the edge of the circular room, and into the Children's Room.

Kyle couldn't make any sense of what he saw:

A white knight.

Two stagehands rolling a chest of drawers on wheels.

A knitter working on a very long Christmas stocking that dragged behind her on the floor.

A plate of eggs colored green.

A girl carrying a shiny purple purse.

An actress dressed up like a witch.

A boy dressed like a poor orphan in one of Charles Dickens's novels, carrying the letter "E."

Three waddling actors in penguin costumes.

A bouquet of daylilies.

An actor wearing a lion costume.

A slice of ham on a plate.

A man pushing a popcorn cart.

A paper moon.

And finally, one of the Alexandriaville reference librarians, Mrs. Maria Simon, carrying a crumpled copy of *Time* magazine.

"Oh-kay," said Kyle. "That was kind of random."

"No," said Sierra, her confidence returning. "It's pretty easy. You just have to put the pieces together. I can do this."

"Good," said Akimi. "Because I sure can't. All I got was *Green Eggs and Ham* by Dr. Seuss."

"What?" said Kyle. "How?"

"Yo," said Miguel. "One dude had a plate of green eggs, another had a slice of ham?"

"Oh. Right."

One by one, the teams sent a player into the Children's Room. When it was Sierra's turn, she went in and quickly came out with her list of book titles and authors:

1. *Goodnight Moon* by Margaret Wise Brown
2. *Green Eggs and Ham* by Dr. Seuss
3. *Lilly's Purple Plastic Purse* by Kevin Henkes
4. *The Lion, the Witch, and the Wardrobe* by C. S. Lewis
5. *Mr. Popper's Penguins* by Richard and Florence Atwater
6. *Pippi Longstocking* by Astrid Lindgren
7. *A Wrinkle in Time* by Madeleine L'Engle

"Whoa," said Akimi. "Wait a second. How'd you get 'Pippi Longstocking'? I remember the lady knitting the 'long stocking,' but how'd you get the 'Pippi' part?"

"Easy," said Sierra. "The Dickensian orphan boy was Pip from *Great Expectations,* and he was carrying the letter 'E,' making him Pip-E or, you know, Pippi."

"Brilliant," said Miguel. "I would've missed that one. I might've missed Mr. Popper, too. He was the guy pushing the popcorn wagon, right?"

Sierra nodded. "And, of course, Mrs. Simon with the crumpled copy of *Time* magazine was *A Wrinkle in Time* by Madeleine L'Engle."

"Nice," said Kyle. "Way to climb back on that horse."

The other seven players eventually put together the same list of titles that Sierra had.

But none of them did it as fast.

The home team picked up the "I Did It!" medal, and just like that, they were back in the lead.

On the fourth day of the competition, however, Kyle and his teammates didn't fare so well.

They lost the Bendable Bookworm medal to the Northeast team after a fierce game of Dewey Decimal Twister. The girl from Rhode Island, Cheryl Space, was extremely flexible.

The Mid-Atlantic team, led by a skinny kid from Maryland named Elliott Schilpp, who could do some serious damage to a plate of food, scored the Eating It Up medal for reading while eating.

In that game, played in the Book Nook Café, each team had to eat pizza while reading a Newbery Honor book from way back in the 1960s that none of the players had ever read before. When the pizza was gone, they had to answer a whole series of comprehension questions. The Mid-Atlantic gang devoured their pepperoni pies the fastest and then nailed every single question about *When Shlemiel Went to Warsaw and Other Stories* by Isaac Bashevis Singer.

Kyle congratulated the kids from Maryland, Virginia, Delaware, and Pennsylvania.

"Thanks," they said, burping up pizza gas.

On the bookmobile ride back to the Olympia Village motel, Kyle realized that, at the end of the fourth day and eighth game, there were only two days and four games left.

Marjory Muldauer and the Midwest team hadn't picked up any new medals on day four, either, so Team Kyle was still in the lead.

The Hometown Heroes had three medals.

The Midwest team, starring Marjory Muldauer, had two.

The Pacific, Mid-Atlantic, and Northeast teams each had one.

"You guys?" said Kyle after doing the mental math. "We only need to win *two more medals* and we're the champions!"

Once again, Miguel started chanting that old song by Queen, "We Are the Champions."

Akimi joined in. Sierra, too.

Then the teammates belted out the chorus in four-part harmony.

"We are the champions, my friend!"

Kyle grinned.

He was definitely looking forward to his next cake day.

30

"What did you and Mrs. Chiltington talk about?" Andrew Peckleman asked Marjory Muldauer.

They were sitting together on the patio near the motel's stone-cold gas-powered fire pit.

"How much we both hate what Mr. Lemoncello's doing at his so-called library. Do you know what insane game they had us play today? Reading while eating."

Andrew shook his head in disbelief.

"And the food was pizza! Greasy, slimy, cheesy pizza!"

"Pizza spillage can cause major damage to books," said Andrew. "I've seen it. Back when I was a library aide at the middle school."

"I complained about the messiness, but Mr. Lemoncello popped in on a video screen to remind us that all the books being used in the read-and-eat contest were paperbacks."

"As if that makes a difference."

"Exactly. Loopy old Lemoncello said paperback books were meant to be taken to the beach, where they'd have suntan lotion, melting ice cream cones, and sand dribbled all over their pages."

"How ridiculous."

"I know. But Lemoncello said books did no one any good sealed up tight. He said books need to 'have their spines cracked, their covers opened, and their pages ruffled for them to come alive.' "

"The man's a menace," said Andrew.

"He's a lunatic."

"He needs to be stopped."

"Don't worry. We're working on it."

"Really? How?"

Marjory studied the nerdy boy in his goggle glasses. Yes, he seemed to be a true library lover, but Marjory couldn't trust him. She couldn't trust anybody—not when the future of library science was at stake.

"I can't say," she told Andrew. "But don't be surprised if Mr. Lemoncello leaves town. I understand he's turned his back on Alexandriaville before."

"Well, he left when he was like eighteen," said Andrew. "He moved to New York City to start his game company."

"And," said Marjory, "from what I've heard, he never once came back here until he cooked up his crazy scheme to build a new library in the old bank building as a big publicity stunt."

"Where'd you hear that?"

"Mrs. Chiltington."

"Huh. Mr. Lemoncello told us he built the library to honor the memory of Mrs. Gail Tobin. The librarian who helped him so much when he was our age."

"Ha! You believe that? That's just the clever spin Mr. Lemoncello's marketing department put on this scam." Marjory stood up. "But don't worry, Andrew. Your public library will soon be a true public library. Mr. Lemoncello will turn it over to a local board of trustees and flee."

"And he won't be coming back?"

"Highly doubtful."

"Wow. Thanks. I guess."

"You're welcome. Excuse me. I need a 641.2."

"Sure. Enjoy your beverage."

Marjory marched into the motel lobby, hoping to find a cold bottle of water. But, of course, the only free beverages the Lemoncello Library Olympics people had put on ice in the open coolers were chocolate milk, strawberry milk, and ten different kinds of soda pop, including something called Mr. Lemoncello's Lemonberry Fizz. All of it junk.

"And a lemon is not a berry, Mr. Lemoncello," Marjory muttered. "Look it up. Six-three-four-point-three-three-four. Lemons as an orchard crop. That means it's a fruit!"

Suddenly, a voice boomed through a megaphone. "Who would like to play another game?"

Mr. Lemoncello. It sounded like he was right outside.

"Will all Library Olympians kindly join me at the swimming pool? It's time to *dive* into another game!"

147

"Come on, Marjory," called Margaret Miles, the Midwest team's coach, hurrying across the lobby. "We're only down by one."

"I thought we were only supposed to play two games per day."

Margaret Miles laughed. "You know Mr. Lemoncello. He's all about keeping things a little unpredictable."

Which is precisely why he shouldn't be allowed anywhere near a library, thought Marjory.

Libraries were all about order, control, precision, and predictability!

And that's exactly how Mrs. Chiltington and her League of Concerned Library Lovers would run things when they became the board of trustees in charge of what used to be the Lemoncello Library.

To help them succeed (and to earn her scholarship from the Willoughby-Chiltington Family Trust), all Marjory had to do was remove one book from the library's shelves.

She had no qualms about it. No doubts or misgivings.

After all, that was what a library was supposed to do: lend out books, not dribble pizza sauce all over their pages.

She planned on borrowing the book Mrs. Chiltington had requested the very next day.

Marjory would earn her "Go to College Free" card.

And if things went the way Mrs. Chiltington said they would, the Alexandriaville Public Library would finally be free of Luigi Lemoncello.

31

"Surprise!" cried Mr. Lemoncello.

Marjory was standing on one side of the motel's swimming pool with the other contestants and their coaches. The blithering buffoon, Mr. Lemoncello, and his head librarian, Dr. Zinchenko, were standing on the other.

"As a library reaches out to the community surrounding it," said the bizarro billionaire, "so do the games of the first Library Olympiad!"

"So we're, like, gonna be playing game number nine right here?" said the blond boy from California, whom Marjory had already decided was an idiot. "Tonight?"

"Absolutamundo," said Mr. Lemoncello. "And although it's not easy being bad, this next game is. Easy, not bad. Then again, I already know all the answers, which makes any quiz easier, wouldn't you agree?"

Dr. Zinchenko tapped a switch box with the toe of her

red high-heeled shoe. An electric air pump *varoom*ed to life to inflate an enormous movie screen that rose beside her like a giant gorilla balloon outside a used-car lot.

"Our ninth game," said Dr. Zinchenko, "is inspired by the Dewey decimal classification 510."

"Mathematics!" shouted Marjory a half second before anybody else.

"Correct," said the librarian. "Solve two of these mathematically inspired picture puzzles before any of the other teams and you will earn our ninth medal, the Rebus!"

"Remember," said Mr. Lemoncello, "you only need two to win, which means we need at least nine puzzles. I think. I'll have to ask Morris, the moose. He's good with math. Anyway, here it is, your first puzzle! Dr. Zinchenko?"

She read from a stack of yellow note cards. "Name this fortress of intellectual freedom fighters."

Mr. Lemoncello snapped his fingers and the fully inflated video screen displayed an equation made up of pictures:

Marjory thought the game was absurd, but her mind went to work anyway. It was like a math equation. LION plus BEAR plus GUY WITH STACK OF BOOKS minus ONE minus CAR equaled what?

No. Wait. The third symbol had to be just one word, like all the others. The guy was carrying the books. CARRY?

Marjory added and subtracted the letters as quickly as she could. She mashed the letters all together: LION-BEARCARRY minus ONECAR.

L I O̶ N̶ B E̶ A R C̶A̶R̶R Y

That left L, I, B, A, R, R, Y.

An extremely easy word jumble.

"A library!" she shouted an instant before Kyle Keeley shouted it, too.

"I heard Miss Muldauer first," said Mr. Lemoncello. "That's one for the Midwest, America's heartland, home of all this great nation's Valentine's Day decorations. Well done!"

Marjory smirked.

If she could figure out one more puzzle, she'd win this game and, once again, be tied for first place.

She no longer needed to win Mr. Lemoncello's Library Olympics for the scholarship money.

But since she was already in the game, she wouldn't mind crushing Kyle Keeley.

32

Kyle was starting to panic.

If Marjory Muldauer solved the next "mathematical" picture puzzle, her team would have *three* medals, just like Team Kyle.

They'd be all tied up.

Again.

And once they were tied, it'd be much easier for the Midwest team to slip into the lead. Kyle's cake day might never come.

"Time for our second mathematically inspired picture puzzle," announced Mr. Lemoncello. "This one is the answer to a trivia question. Dr. Zinchenko, if you please?"

Dr. Zinchenko read a question off another yellow card. "In the year AD 35, the Roman emperor Caligula tried to ban a book because it expressed Greek ideals of freedom, which Caligula did not like, because Rome was occupying

152

Greece at the time. Which book did the Roman emperor try to ban?"

A new image filled the inflated screen:

Kyle stared at the second puzzle.

He needed to decipher it, fast. No way was he letting Marjory Muldauer snag this one, too.

Three home runs minus the symbol for the United Nations.

That had to be HOME RUNS minus UN, or HOMERS!

"I think I know this," whispered Sierra.

Kyle's world shifted into super slow motion. In his head, he heard Miguel saying, "I think the answer is *Flubber*." The last time a game was on the line and Kyle listened to someone who "thought" they knew the answer, he'd lost. To his mom. And that was just a board game. This was way more important.

Kyle ignored Sierra. Made his mind race as fast as it could. He was the team's "game guy." That was what everybody kept telling him back when he had wanted to quit. Well, this puzzle was a game. It was his job to win it, no matter what.

THEATER minus EAT minus R equaled THE.

The last two lines were the hardest

ODD (numbers) minus D plus GOAL minus E plus a backward GOAL, or LAOG, equaled ODGOALLAOG.

Sierra tried to get Kyle's attention again. "Caligula was the Roman emperor in AD 35 and the book he banned was—"

"Hang on," said Kyle. "I just need to unscramble the last jumble."

"Yo, Kyle?" said Miguel. "Sierra has the answer."

"So do I," said Kyle. He turned to face Dr. Zinchenko and hollered, "Homer's *The Good Ol Gala*!"

"Wha-hut?" said Akimi the second Kyle blurted it out.

"Sorry," said Dr. Zinchenko, "that answer is incorrect."

"Homer's *The Odyssey*," said Marjory very coolly.

"Ha! That's wrong!" cried Kyle. "She didn't even use the 'G,' 'O,' 'A,' or 'L' from 'goal'!"

"Of course I didn't," said Marjory. "Because I believe that symbol is supposed to represent the word 'yes,' which backward would be 's-e-y.' But I didn't need the puzzle pictures. I knew the answer because, unlike some people, I've actually read a few history books."

"That's how I knew it, too," sighed Sierra.

"Ms. Muldauer's answer is correct," said Mr. Lemoncello. "The Midwest team has won two out of two, and therefore, they have also won the Rebus medal. And, if my own mental math is correct, the Midwest team now has three medals, which equals the same number currently held by the hometown team. It's a three-for-all! A tie! Wow, isn't math marvelous?"

"Way to go, *mon capitaine*," said Akimi, knuckle-punching Kyle in the arm. "Next time, try to remember you're on a *team*."

Kyle and his teammates, along with all the other Library Olympians, were allowed to sleep in the next morning, because thanks to the surprise poolside contest, there would be only one game played that day.

Of course, Kyle didn't want to sleep in. He wanted to get back in the arena ASAP and retake the lead.

He didn't like being tied with Marjory Muldauer.

He didn't like knowing his team had lost the poolside pop quiz because he'd blurted out the wrong answer and hadn't let Sierra say the right one.

He also didn't like being *this close* to losing.

Kyle and Miguel were sitting in the Olympia Village dining room, pushing the bobbing yellow marshmallows around in their Lucky Lemoncello Lumps cereal bowls.

"Sorry about blowing it last night," he said to Miguel.

"Don't apologize to me. Tell Sierra."

"I will. But now we still have to win *two* of the last three games."

"Not necessarily, bro. If one of the teams with no medals or just one medal beats us, we're still in a tie with—"

"Miguel?" Kyle snapped. "We *need* to win two more games."

"Yo. Ease up, Kyle."

"Ease up? If we lose this thing, do you know what people are going to say about us? That we just got lucky the first time. That Charles Chiltington probably would've won the escape game if Mr. Lemoncello hadn't kicked him out on a technicality."

"Yeah. They might say that. Or they might say, 'You win some, you lose some.' But what counts is how you play the game."

"Well, I am not playing to lose, Miguel."

"Hey, neither am I. And I'm not playing alone."

"I know. And we need you to step it up a little."

"What?"

"You're the only member of our team who hasn't won a single medal."

"Gee, Kyle, thanks for reminding me."

"Have you guys seen Marjory Muldauer?" asked Akimi as she and Sierra joined the boys at the breakfast table. "I like to keep my eye on our competition at all times."

"What about all these other kids?" said Sierra, gesturing to the tables filled with the country's top young bibliophiles. "They're our competition, too."

Akimi blew that off with a wave of her hand.

"Come on, Sierra. Little Miss Library from Michigan has won every single one of the Midwest team's medals for them. She's our only real threat. Especially if Kyle keeps hogging the ball and missing his shots."

Kyle sighed. "I'm really sorry about shouting out the wrong answer last night, Sierra."

"Apology accepted," said Sierra. "Next time, maybe you could, I don't know, trust me?"

Kyle nodded. "Definitely."

Akimi craned her neck and checked out all the other tables. "So where is Marjory?"

"She went to the library early," said Andrew Peckleman, who was rolling a rubber barrel between tables to collect people's breakfast trash. "She wanted to do some studying, so my uncle drove her over there."

"What's she studying?" asked Kyle.

"How to beat you," whined Andrew.

"And how's she going to do that, Andrew? What'd she find to study at the library when none of us even know what the tenth game is going to be?"

"I don't know. Do I look like a mind reader?"

"No, Andrew, I'd say you look like a garbage man."

"Kyle?" said Sierra, shaking her head. "That wasn't nice."

"In fact," said Akimi, "it was downright nasty."

"Yeah," said Miguel, with his arms crossed over his chest. "What is with you today?"

"Sorry, Andrew," said Kyle. "I'm just a little on edge."

"Well, you should be," said Andrew, adjusting his goggle glasses. "Because Marjory Muldauer is going to kick your butt, and I can't wait to watch her kicking it. Now, if you will excuse me, I have more garbage to collect."

Andrew pushed his barrel away.

Akimi glared at Kyle. Sierra stirred her cereal. Miguel shook his head.

"Andrew's a decent guy, Kyle," said Miguel, sounding disappointed. "He didn't deserve that."

"I know. I'm sorry. We just really, *really* need to win today's game—whatever it is."

34

The library was extra packed with spectators for the fifth day of the Olympic games.

Television cameras were everywhere.

Word must've spread that unless one of the other medaled teams miraculously swept the final three competitions, the championship was down to two true contenders.

"Welcome back, everybody!" said Mr. Lemoncello, addressing the contestants and the crowd from the second-floor balcony, where he was seated in a canvas director's chair. He was wearing a floppy beret and an ascot like movie directors sometimes do—in cartoons. "I hope you're all having fun!"

"Fun?" shouted Mrs. Chiltington, who was back, once again, with her pack of protestors. "Libraries should be about books, Mr. Lemoncello. Not fun!"

Even from a distance, Kyle could see some kind of dark cloud shadow his hero's eyes.

"Good to see you again, too, Archduchess Von Chiltington. And may I say, for the record, as well as the CD, I agree with thee."

"Ha! Prove it."

"My pleasure." He turned to address the assembled Library Olympians. "Today, for game number ten of the duodecimalthon, we'll do a little role-playing. You Olympians will play librarians, and I will play the patron who has come here seeking a very particular, very special *book*."

He shot Mrs. Chiltington a toothy smile, then pivoted back to the players.

"But I can't remember the title or the author or whether this *book* . . . "

Another smile for Mrs. Chiltington, who wasn't smiling back.

". . . is fiction or nonfiction. Your mission, should you choose to accept it, is to find this one needle in our haystack of five million different titles."

Mr. Lemoncello whipped off the beret and tugged on an Ohio State Buckeyes baseball cap.

"I will now play the patron. Before I do, however, I'd like to express my sincere gratitude to my brilliant acting coach, the renowned thespian Sir Donald Thorne, for his assistance in helping me craft my portrayal of this role."

Mr. Lemoncello cleared this throat and started speaking with a flat and friendly Ohio accent.

"Excuse me, Ms. and/or Mr. Librarian, can you help me find a book? All I remember is that it's kind of white and brownish on the front. It might be about the opposite of wildlife mixed up with a James Joyce novel, but Joyce didn't write it, although I think a woman did. I also remember something about a fruit no one has ever heard of before the year 2014. It's about yea thick. The book. Not the fruit. Can you please find it for me? Right away?"

Mr. Lemoncello whipped off the baseball cap and put the director's beret back on.

"The first team to locate the book and bring it to me wins our tenth medal, the Thank You medal. You will also, of course, win your patron's eternal gratitude. Okay, maybe not eternal, but he'll probably say 'thanks' when you hand him the book. Maybe. They do that, sometimes."

The thirty-two players stood frozen, staring up at Mr. Lemoncello.

Mr. Lemoncello didn't say anything else.

"Is that it?" asked Stephanie Youngerman from Boise, Idaho.

"Yes," said Dr. Zinchenko, stepping up to the railing on the second floor beside Mr. Lemoncello.

Then she was silent, too.

"Okay, you guys," Kyle whispered to his teammates. "Let's get busy."

"What should we do first?" asked Sierra.

"Weep," said Akimi. "That's the lamest clue I've ever heard."

"Nuh-uh," said Miguel. "I have a few ideas."

Kyle and his teammates headed to a desk in the outer ring so they could converse privately.

Marjory Muldauer led her team to a desk on the opposite side of the circle. Pretty soon, all the teams were grabbing desks and firing up the tablet computers built into the furniture so they could explore the library's online card catalog.

"So what fruit was first discovered in 2014?" asked Akimi, zeroing in on that part of the clue. "Craisins?"

"Hold up," said Miguel. "You're being too literal."

"Miguel's right," said Kyle. "Mr. Lemoncello is way too wacky to mean exactly what he said."

"So what *are* we looking for?" asked Sierra. "A new apple? A new banana? A new strawberry?"

"Bingo!" said Miguel. "That's it!" He started tapping the built-in tablet computer's screen.

Sierra was stunned. "Really? What'd I say?"

" 'New strawberry,' " said Akimi. "Which, I'm sorry, but I don't really think is a 'bingo' kind of answer."

"Because," said Miguel, as quietly as he could, "we don't need a new strawberry. We need a different kind of 'new berry.' "

"Which one?" said Kyle. "Blueberry? Raspberry?"

Akimi snapped her fingers. "Huckleberry! Because this is a library and *Huckleberry Finn* is in here."

163

"No, you guys." Miguel found a stubby pencil and a slip of scrap paper. "The 2014 Newbery Medal winner. *Flora and Ulysses* by Kate DiCamillo."

Akimi's eyes lit up. " 'Flora,' meaning 'vegetation,' is the opposite of 'fauna,' meaning 'wildlife.' "

"And," added Sierra, "James Joyce, the great Irish novelist, wrote a book called *Ulysses*."

"And Kate DiCamillo sounds like a lady's name that isn't Joyce," said Kyle.

"Triple bingo," said Miguel, scrolling through the card catalog entry for the book. "Dang."

"What?"

"All the copies in the Children's Room are checked out."

"Did they also put a copy on the fiction shelves?" asked Sierra.

"Yes! Just one. I guess so adults can check it out, too. That means the only copy in the whole building is right over there."

Miguel head-bobbed toward the bookcases that wrapped around the back third of the Rotunda Reading Room and climbed all the way up to the base of the Wonder Dome.

"We're gonna need a hover ladder," said Kyle.

"And this code." Miguel showed his teammates a slip of paper with "F.D545f 2013" written on it.

"Punch it into the hover ladder pad!" Akimi said to Miguel. "Go get our book."

"No way," said Miguel. "I'm scared of heights. *You* do it, Akimi."

"No way. Go on, Kyle."

Kyle shook his head. "You guys were right this morning. I don't want to be a 'ball hog' again."

"This ball you can hog. Go!"

"Hurry," said Sierra. "I think some of the other teams just figured it out, too."

35

Kyle dashed across the marble floor.

So did Stephanie Youngerman, the girl from Boise.

And Elliott Schilpp, the skinny genius from Maryland who had won the pizza-eating contest.

Uh-oh, thought Kyle. *The Mid-Atlantic team already has one medal. If they win this game, they actually have a shot at being crowned champions.*

Kyle ran faster. Fortunately, there were eight hover ladders, one for each team, lined up under the three-story-tall bookcases.

"Only one ladder per team," announced Dr. Zinchenko.

The instant she did, each of the other teams sent someone scurrying over to float up the fiction wall. Even if they didn't know what book they were looking for, they knew it wasn't in any of the Dewey decimal rooms now that the hover ladders had more or less been declared game pieces.

Kyle reached for a hover ladder.

But Marjory Muldauer grabbed its handles first.

"Sorry, Keeley. This ride is taken."

So were the next three down in either direction. Thanks to Marjory Muldauer, Kyle would have to dash to the very end of the line.

He ran past Stephanie Youngerman, who was furiously tapping in the winning code on her hover ladder's control pad.

Elliott Schilpp was jabbing in a number, too.

Stephanie Youngerman lifted off first.

By the time Kyle reached his hover ladder and typed in the book code and waited for the safety boots to clamp shut around his shins, three other teams were already floating up the wall: Mountain, Mid-Atlantic, and, of course, Marjory Muldauer for Midwest.

Kyle's platform finally drifted up from the floor and set off on a diagonal tangent for the 2014 Newbery Medal winner—and a very possible midair collision with the three other players, who were all aiming for the same target.

To his left, Kyle heard keys clacking.

Marjory Muldauer was typing a different code into her pad.

Her hover ladder stuttered to a stop, then shot sideways at a forty-five-degree angle. Kyle stayed on his direct trajectory to *Flora and Ulysses,* but within seconds, his hover ladder's infrared collision sensors picked up the approach of Marjory's platform.

"Yield to traffic," cooed a computerized voice from the tiny speaker in Kyle's control panel.

Marjory thumbed her red emergency stop button.

Her hover ladder froze, right where it would block Kyle's ascent.

"Yield to traffic." His hover ladder's safety features had put him in a lockdown mode.

Marjory pretended to be studying the books in front of her.

"That's not where the book we're looking for is and you know it!" Kyle shouted at her.

Marjory didn't say a word. In fact, she looked a little airsick.

Kyle twisted his body so he could see around Marjory's stalled ladder and watch the final seconds of the race to F.D545f 2013.

Stephanie Youngerman's hover ladder screeched to a halt and she shot out her arm to grab the book.

Then she started sliding books around on the shelf. Shoving them sideways. Looking behind them.

"I'm here!" she shouted. "But the book isn't."

The crowd of spectators gasped.

Mr. Lemoncello surprised all the floaters by swinging open a window-sized door cut into the bookcases. He poked his head out maybe three feet away from where *Flora and Ulysses* was supposed to be shelved. "I beg your pardon?"

"*Flora and Ulysses,*" said Stephanie Youngerman.

"The 2014 Newbery winner. It's not here. Kate DiCamillo's other books are. *Because of Winn-Dixie*. *The Tale of Despereaux*. But there's only an empty gap where *Flora and Ulysses* is supposed to be."

"But this is impossible," said Mr. Lemoncello. "Dr. Zinchenko? Don't we have two dozen copies of that book?"

"Three, sir," said Dr. Zinchenko after popping open another window in the bookcase. "They are all checked out. That was our last copy."

"This is preposterous!" declared Mrs. Chiltington, striding forward to the front of the viewer gallery on the first floor. Her son Charles and a group of well-dressed ladies and one gentleman in a bow tie pushed their way forward with her.

"Missing books? Silly dinosaur video games? Money wasted on talking statues and holograms and secret panels in bookcases that could've been more wisely spent on extra copies of popular children's books?"

Mrs. Chiltington propped her hands on her hips and scowled up at Mr. Lemoncello.

"This library is a disgrace, sir. An absolute disgrace!"

"Perhaps you are right, Contessa Chiltington," said Mr. Lemoncello, sounding extremely sad—something Kyle had never heard him sound before. "A library without books? That is, indeed, a disgrace. An absolute disgrace."

36

Kyle watched Mr. Lemoncello halfheartedly award the Thank You medal to the Mountain team.

But his mind drifted back to the hover ladder race.

Marjory Muldauer had blocked him on purpose. She wasn't even trying to go for the book.

Why'd she do that? he wondered. *Why'd she want the Mountain team to win this round?*

"Hip, hip, hooray," said Mr. Lemoncello as he limply shook the winner's hand. "You won the tenth medal. Yippee, huzzah, and various other exclamations of glee. You were the first to reach the empty slot where the winning book should've been, which makes me want to sing, *'Brown bear, brown bear, what do you see? An empty hole where a book ought to be.'*"

Mr. Lemoncello turned to face the crowd.

"Thank you, Library Olympians and library lovers, for

170

joining us here today. Come back tomorrow for the final two games of the first Library Olympics. Now go away! All of you! Go!"

The crowd was stunned into silence.

The control room crew quickly pumped show tunes through all the speakers under the dome to cover the awkward silence. The ten holographic statues ringing the rotunda turned into the Trapp Family Singers and Uncle Max from *The Sound of Music*. They waved cheerfully and sang, *"So long, farewell, auf Wiedersehen, goodbye!"*

"That concludes today's competition," said the soothing lady's voice in the ceiling. "The score, after ten of the twelve games of the first Library Olympiad's duodecimalthon: Pacific, Northeast, Mid-Atlantic, and Mountain teams—one medal. The Midwest team and the Hometown Heroes—three medals."

"So," said John Sazaklis, the anchor for the Book Network's live coverage of the games, "it seems we're looking at a battle of the bookworms between the two top teams. They're all tied up, three to three. And there are only two games left."

"That's right," said his sidekick, renowned librarian Helen Burnham. "Of course, one of the four teams with a single medal could dazzle us all and sweep the final two competitions. It's still possible that this thing could end in a three-way tie."

"Exciting."

"You betcha, John. There's only one thing we know

for certain. The South will not rise again. Both the Southeast and the Southwest teams have remained medal-less in these games. I'm afraid those kids have no chance at being declared Mr. Lemoncello's library champions."

"Too bad. I really like their cowboy hats and NASCAR tracksuits."

37

A half hour later, the library was empty except for Team Kyle, Mr. Lemoncello, Dr. Zinchenko, and the engineers locked behind the red door in the library's control room.

Kyle and his friends wanted to be there for Mr. Lemoncello in what looked like his hour of despair.

"I'm sure whoever checked out *Flora and Ulysses* is enjoying it immensely," said Sierra Russell. "I know I did."

"Thank you, Sierra," said Mr. Lemoncello, who was breaking his own library rules, spooning a half gallon of ice cream straight out of its carton while he sat slumped in one of the comfortable reading chairs at the base of the fiction wall. He wore a bib to stop the ice cream from dribbling on his clothes.

"You're really only supposed to eat food in the Book Nook Café, sir," said Miguel.

Mr. Lemoncello ignored Miguel and shoveled up another gob of birthday-cake ice cream.

Meanwhile, Dr. Zinchenko had commandeered a hover ladder and sailed up to the spot where the missing book should've been shelved.

"The book was here last week," said Dr. Zinchenko, examining the gap between Kate DiCamillo titles. "I know it was. I made certain of it, right before we locked down the library to the public. Since then, the only ones allowed near the books have been our thirty-two young Olympians. . . ."

"Fascinating," said Mr. Lemoncello, not sounding fascinated at all. He shoveled more confetti-sprinkled ice cream into his mouth.

Dr. Zinchenko started her slow descent. "I must talk to security about this."

"Don't bother, Dr. Zinchenko," said Mr. Lemoncello. "This is a library. Books check in but they don't check out. No, wait. That's a Roach Motel. I forget what happens at a library. Maybe Mrs. Chiltington is correct. Maybe we should find some more mature adults to run this place. We really had three dozen copies of that same title and now they're all gone?"

"Yes, sir."

Mr. Lemoncello heaved a heavy sigh.

"This is horrible," shrieked the holographic librarian Mrs. Gause, as once again she flickered to frazzled life behind the circulation desk. "This is what happened last time! First, books started disappearing. History books. One title in particular. All ten copies. Nobody cared. The whole town turned its back on its library. Very important people convinced the mayor to cut our funding. Before long, you couldn't even find a bookmark or an empty jar of library paste. Then *BOOM!* Here come the bulldozers and the wrecking ball! So long, library; hello, parking lot. Oh, the horror. The horror."

"Thank you, Mrs. Gause," said Mr. Lemoncello, gobbling down his ice cream even faster. "Good to hear from you again. Control room?"

Mr. Lemoncello flicked his wrist.

The hologram vanished.

Kyle approached his hero.

"Do you need anything, Mr. Lemoncello? Anything at all."

Mr. Lemoncello looked up from his tub of ice cream. The twinkle was gone from his coal-black eyes.

"Just what I've been looking for all along, Kyle. My true champions."

"Don't worry, sir. We won't let you down. We'll win both of the last two medals. I promise."

Mr. Lemoncello looked at Kyle, shook his head, and sighed again.

38

The Hometown Heroes' bookmobile ride from Olympia Village to the Lemoncello Library the following morning was as dreary as the weather.

Kyle and his teammates stared out the rain-streaked windows and watched familiar streets roll by.

"How weird will it be," said Akimi, "if the next time we head downtown to the library, we're not famous anymore? What if we're just a bunch of losers?"

"Thanks for that inspirational thought, Akimi," said Miguel. "You should really consider a career as a motivational speaker."

"What if something worse happens?" said Sierra. "What if all that stuff Mrs. Gause mentioned happens again? What if Mr. Lemoncello decides to close his library?"

"Why would he do that?" asked Kyle.

"Because he's tired of people taking out books and not bringing them back. He looked so sad yesterday."

"Yo," said Miguel. "He's a bazillionaire. He can always buy more books."

"You guys?" said Kyle. "Dr. Zinchenko said the *Flora and Ulysses* book was in its spot on the fiction shelf a week ago. And no one has been able to check books out since then except—"

"The thirty-two Library Olympians!" said Akimi, finishing Kyle's sentence, the way friends sometimes do.

"Yo!" said Miguel. "That means somebody on one of the other teams took the book out of the library. One of the kids Mr. Lemoncello spent so much time and energy searching for."

"No wonder he was so upset about a single missing book," said Sierra.

"Yep," said Kyle. "One of his specially selected library nerds stole that book." He turned to Miguel. "No offense."

"None taken."

When the team trooped up the slick marble steps into the library's lobby, they saw Charles Chiltington, his mother, a bunch of stuffy-looking ladies, and that one guy in a bow tie. This time, they were ringed around the Mr. Lemoncello fountain, which wasn't gurgling water like it was supposed to.

Each member of Mrs. Chiltington's crew was carrying a one-word protest sign. Together, they read "Is THIS ANY

LIBRARY? WAY TO RUN A." Bow-tie man, who was holding the "LIBRARY?" placard, was standing in the wrong spot.

Kyle and his teammates lingered in the archway just long enough to hear what Mrs. Chiltington and Charles were saying to the Book Network reporter interviewing them.

"If this library is to be a true public institution," said Charles's mother, "then it requires public oversight. It should be governed by a board of community trustees, not by a one-man band."

"Especially," said Charles, "when the batty bandleader is a disingenuous and mendacious charlatan."

"Are you suggesting that Mr. Lemoncello is both a liar and a fraud?" asked the reporter.

"Heavens no," said Charles. "Don't be preposterous."

"But that's what those words you just used mean."

"Charles is simply upset," said Mrs. Chiltington, draping a protective arm around her son. "That's why we're here today. Our children deserve a proper library, not an indoor amusement park. Mr. Lemoncello is exposing their impressionable minds to things such as a smell-a-vision version of some book called *Walter the Farting Dog* that children and their impressionable noses simply should not be exposed to."

Then she smiled and blinked. Repeatedly.

Kyle and his teammates shook their heads and continued into the Rotunda Reading Room.

"Hey, Kyle!"

It was his brother Mike.

"Don't disappoint us!"

And his other brother, Curtis.

"Win, baby, win!" screamed Mike, pumping his arm. "Woo-hoo! O-H, I-O! O-H, I-O!"

They were with Kyle's mom and dad in the capacity crowd that was bunched behind velvet ropes for the final two events of the duodecimalthon. So was everybody else's family. And friends. It seemed like the whole town of Alexandriaville had turned out for the big finale.

"No pressure or anything," said Akimi.

"Yo," said Miguel, pointing up at the Wonder Dome. "Check it out. I bet they did that to cheer up Mr. Lemoncello."

"I was hoping there might be balloons," said Kyle as he admired the ceiling.

"It's beautiful," said Sierra.

It looked like Dr. Zinchenko had instructed her video artists to run a Balloon Fiesta simulation for the final day of the Library Olympics. The Wonder Dome had been magically transformed into a brilliant blue sky filled with brightly colored hot-air balloons. The video loop made the Rotunda Reading Room feel as if it were a gondola gently swaying beneath a motley-colored airship drifting along on a warm breeze.

It was awesome.

"Turn! It! Off!" decreed a voice from the third-floor balcony.

Kyle looked up. Mr. Lemoncello stood at the railing. He was dressed in a black suit, black shirt, and black tie. He looked like he was on his way to a funeral.

The Wonder Dome went dark. It was just a curved white ceiling.

"I was so looking forward to this day," sighed Mr. Lemoncello from his lofty perch. "Today is the day I thought I would finally discover my true champions."

He looked down at the thirty-two Library Olympians.

Kyle thought he knew why his hero seemed so sad. One, or maybe more, of the thirty-two kids Mr. Lemoncello had entrusted with all the wonders of his library had betrayed him. They had taken away a book they weren't supposed to even touch.

"But instead of being giddy," Mr. Lemoncello continued, "I feel like a Watership. Down. Dr. Zinchenko? Will you kindly run game eleven? My internal Olympic torch is dimming and is in desperate need of fresh batteries. Therefore, I will be in my private suite working on the clues for game twelve, the final and most important game of the Lemoncello Library Olympics."

Mr. Lemoncello waved a feeble wave and disappeared into his private suite on the third floor.

Dr. Zinchenko, also dressed in black—a shiny, short leather dress—strode into the Rotunda Reading Room. Even her glasses had black frames instead of their usual red ones.

"Will the following teams please choose a representative for the eleventh game of our duodecimalthon: the Midwest, the Northeast, the Mid-Atlantic, the Mountain team, the Pacific team, and the local team from Alexandriaville, Ohio."

Marjory Muldauer shot her arm into the air.

"Yes, Miss Muldauer?"

"What's this game going to be about? Drinking milk shakes while floating books in a hot tub?"

"No, Miss Muldauer, although your sarcasm is duly noted. Game eleven will celebrate your freedom to express yourself with snarky scorn as well as everyone else's freedom to read. Today's first game will be all about *banned* books."

39

Sierra turned to her teammates. "Who should play for us?"

"Either you or Miguel," said Kyle.

"Definitely," agreed Akimi.

"I vote for Sierra," said Miguel. "You've read more books than the rest of us combined."

"Are you guys sure? Because I didn't do so well in that Battle of the Books game."

"And I did terribly in the poolside puzzle fiasco," said Kyle. "Remember?"

Sierra smiled. "I may never forget it."

"Yeah. Me neither. Come on. You'll be great. I don't know anything about band books. Did John Philip Sousa write one?"

"*Banned* books," said Sierra.

"See? You're doing better than me already."

"Teams?" said Dr. Zinchenko. "Please send your designated player to the circle of desks closest to mine."

Sierra looked at her teammates one last time. They were all smiling and nodding. She started walking to the inner ring of reading desks.

"Go, Sierra!"

That was her dad. Cheering for her.

"Good luck, honey!"

Her mom, too.

Each of the six remaining teams was assigned its own desk. Sierra sat down at hers. Marjory Muldauer was at the desk to her right. Elliott Schilpp, the nice guy from Maryland who really liked pizza, was on her left.

Each desk had its own built-in touch-screen computer.

"This contest will include an immediate elimination factor," announced Dr. Zinchenko from her swivel stool behind the central librarian's desk. "If you answer a question incorrectly, you will be asked to leave your desk. Quietly. As those of you playing for the Northeast, the Mid-Atlantic, the Mountain, and the Pacific teams undoubtedly recall, you only have one medal each. If you are eliminated from this game, it will be mathematically impossible for your team to go on and win the duodecimalthon. Therefore, if you lose, your team loses its chance at being crowned champions."

The four players nodded. They all understood the very high stakes of this eleventh game.

"However," said Dr. Zinchenko, "should you win this game as well as our twelfth game, we will have a three-way tie for first place and enter into a sudden-death overtime situation. That thirteenth game, if necessary, will take place tomorrow."

"Don't worry," sneered Marjory. "We won't be playing any games tomorrow."

"Let us begin," said Dr. Zinchenko, completely ignoring Marjory Muldauer. "I will read a multiple-choice question. Use the touch-screen computers in your reading desks to select your answer."

Sierra took in a deep breath.

"Question number one: In 1985, Shel Silverstein's *A Light in the Attic* was banned from a school in Wisconsin because:

    a) the attic was cluttered and dangerous.
    b) the children in the book were filthy and
       never combed their hair.
    c) the book encouraged children to break dishes
       so they wouldn't have to dry them.
    d) the book used foul language.

Please enter your answer now."

Sierra had read about this book-banning incident. She tapped "C." Her computer screen glowed green. She was correct.

The Northeast and Mountain teams, however, chose

184

the wrong answer. The screens on their computers turned bright red.

"Thank you for playing," said Dr. Zinchenko. "Kindly rejoin your teammates. And thank you for participating in the first-ever Library Olympiad. You and your teammates will receive lovely parting gifts."

"Whoop-de-doo," said Marjory. "Next question, please."

"Of course. Question number two: Why was Dr. Seuss's book *The Lorax* banned?

a) There is no such creature as a Lorax.
b) The drawings were too frightening for young readers.
c) The rhymes and silly names were too weird.
d) It offended forestry workers.

Choose your answer now. You have thirty seconds."

Sierra wasn't certain about this one. The first three answers could be reasons to ban *any* Dr. Seuss book. But *The Lorax* was all about "Truffula" trees and saving the environment. Forestry workers might not like that.

She went with "D."

Her touch screen glowed green.

So did Marjory Muldauer's.

The Pacific team answered incorrectly.

"Sorry," Sierra said to Pranav Pillai as he left his table. "Thanks. Good luck!"

"Three players remain," said Dr. Zinchenko. "Here is your third question: Why was Junie B. Jones, a series of children's books by Barbara Park, banned from libraries? Was it because:

a) Junie B. Jones is a mouthy brat?
b) characters use words such as 'stupid' and 'dumb'?
c) the author takes liberties with traditional spelling?
d) the main character makes bad choices?
e) all of the above?"

Since Sierra had loved the Junie B. books when she was younger, she knew the correct answer was "E) all of the above."

So did Marjory Muldauer.

Elliott Schilpp, however, did not. His red screen meant the Mid-Atlantic team was out of the competition.

It also meant the whole Library Olympics came down to the Hometown Heroes versus the Midwest.

Sierra Russell versus Marjory Muldauer.

40

"And then there were two!" shouted Mr. Lemoncello from his third-floor balcony. "This finale is far too exciting to miss!"

"Are you feeling better, sir?" asked Dr. Zinchenko.

"Much!" He looked down at Sierra and Marjory. "I've been watching you two on TV! There's nothing like a pair of brilliant young minds set free in a library to perk me up! Plus, I've decided to hire detective Sammy Keyes, who found the hotel thief, to help me find the book thief, which, of course, is now available on DVD in our movie department on the first floor."

He scampered down the spiral staircases.

Kyle heard a funny *burp-squeak-burp* sound and smiled. Mr. Lemoncello was still dressed all in black, but he'd put on his banana shoes.

As he made his way around and around and down the

two flights of curling, corkscrewing steps, his shoes were honking out a song: "The Wheels on the Bus Go Round and Round."

Good, thought Kyle. His hero was back!

Mr. Lemoncello sprinted to the center of the Rotunda Reading Room, leapt up, and somersaulted over the librarian's desk. When he landed on the other side, his banana shoes let out a gassy *PPPFFFFFIIP.*

The audience laughed, applauded, and cheered.

Well, everybody except Mrs. Chiltington and her friends. Kyle could see them shaking their heads disgustedly.

"I'll take over from here, Dr. Zinchenko!" said Mr. Lemoncello.

"Very well, sir." She handed him her stack of question cards.

"Hello, Sierra."

"Hello, sir."

"Marjory."

She waggled her fingers at him like she was bored.

"Okeydokey, pokey," said Mr. Lemoncello. "You two look lonely. Teammates? Come on down."

Kyle, Akimi, and Miguel dashed down the aisle between desks to join Sierra.

"I'm good," said Marjory, stopping her teammates in their tracks. "I don't need any help."

"Very well," said Mr. Lemoncello. "Let me recap."

He reached under the librarian's desk and pulled out

a purple flower-petal swim cap, which he tugged down snugly over his curly white hair.

"Your two teams are currently tied, with three medals each. We have two games remaining: this one and then the one that comes after it, which would be the next one. This is extremely exciting, wouldn't you agree?"

"Yes, sir," said Kyle and his teammates.

Marjory Muldauer shrugged. "Can we move on to the next question?"

"Moving on," said Mr. Lemoncello. "This next question is not—I repeat, *not*—a multiple guess. You must tap in your answer using the keypad on your tabletop's tablet computer. We're still in the category of banned books, only this time they're more than banned, because these poor books were burned. Here is your question: On what date did the Dominican priest Savonarola collect and publicly burn thousands of lewd books in Florence, Italy?"

Kyle looked at Sierra.

She nodded.

"Go for it," said Kyle.

Sierra typed in her answer: SHROVE TUESDAY, 1497.

Kyle could hear the computer's *click-clack* sound effects accompanying Marjory's glass-tapping as she entered her answer, too.

"Is that your final answer, Sierra?" asked Mr. Lemoncello.

"Yes, sir."

"Miss Muldauer?"

"Well, duh. I typed it in, didn't I?"

"Indeed you did. Dr. Zinchenko?"

"The answer we were looking for is Shrove Tuesday, 1497!"

"Woo-hoo!" shouted Kyle.

"That's the answer Sierra Russell gave me," said Mr. Lemoncello, checking his own computer screen. "Miss Muldauer, I'm afraid your answer is incorrect."

"No, it's not."

"I'm sorry, Miss Muldauer," said Dr. Zinchenko. "You did not type in 'Shrove Tuesday, 1497.'"

"I know. Because that answer isn't specific enough."

"I beg your pardon?" said Mr. Lemoncello, taking off his bathing cap. "My ears were covered by rubberized flower petals. Are you saying my head librarian, Dr. Yanina Zinchenko, has incorrectly identified the answer as 'Shrove Tuesday, 1497?'"

"It's an okay answer," said Marjory. "If you're lazy. My answer, however, is more correct. February 7, 1497. Yes, it was also Shrove Tuesday, now commonly referred to as Mardi Gras, but your question specifically asked for a *date*, not a day."

The whole crowd gasped.

Kyle could feel his heart racing in his chest.

Was Sierra's answer technically incorrect?

If so, did that mean his team lost another medal?

"This is quite the quizzical, perplexable, and curious conundrum," said Mr. Lemoncello. "Fortunately, we are in a library, where librarians may not know everything but they certainly know how to find it. Dr. Zinchenko?"

"I will go upstairs to the triple zero room, locate the appropriate encyclopedia volume, and check both 'Savonarola' and 'Shrove Tuesday.'"

"Aha. Might I suggest you start with the 'S' volume?"

"Such was my plan, sir."

"Excellent pre-research planning, Dr. Zinchenko. We wait with bated breath, so kindly hurry before things get too fishy down here."

Heels clicking on the marble floor, Dr. Zinchenko made her way to the nearest spiral staircase, then clanked up the steps to the second floor.

Mr. Lemoncello turned to the closest television camera. "Don't go away. We'll be right back with the correct answer to our last question right after this word from our sponsors."

"This is public TV," whispered the camera operator. "We don't do commercials."

"Oh. Well, can't you do a pledge drive or something? Or should I just make funny faces?"

"Funny faces would be fine, sir."

While Mr. Lemoncello mugged for the camera, Miguel turned to his teammates. "Dr. Z is headed upstairs for the zero-three-zeros. That's the Dewey decimal classification for encyclopedias and books of facts."

"Actually," said Marjory, leaning back smugly, "she will be looking for zero-three-*two*, encyclopedias in American

191

English. You people need to start being much more specific; otherwise—"

Suddenly, there was a shriek from the second floor.

Dr. Zinchenko raced to the balcony railing. "They're gone!"

"What?" cried Mr. Lemoncello.

"All the 'S' encyclopedias, sir. They're missing. Every single one!"

"What? How is that possible?"

"I don't know, sir. We never check out encyclopedias. Somebody must have stolen them!"

Kyle was sort of relieved.

If the encyclopedias Dr. Zinchenko needed were missing, maybe they'd just move on to another question. Hopefully, another one Sierra knew the answer to.

"Guess we need to move on to the next question card," Kyle said to Mr. Lemoncello.

"Not so fast, Keeley," said Marjory. "Since Mr. Lemoncello was so sweet to give us smartphones when we played that Battle of the Books game, I used mine to Google 'Bonfire of the Vanities, 1497,' because that's what the Italians used to call the burning of objects they considered immoral. If I may quote: 'The most infamous bonfire took place on *February seventh, 1497,* when the Dominican priest Savonarola collected and publicly burned thousands of objects like art and books in Florence, Italy, on the day of the Mardi Gras festival.' It doesn't even mention Shrove

Tuesday. It does, however, confirm that my answer, February seventh, 1497, is correct."

Perched on a stool behind the librarian's desk, Mr. Lemoncello looked completely dumbfounded.

Miguel pointed at Marjory. "You used your phone to find the answer! You cheated."

"No, I did not. I only used it to *confirm* my answer."

"I am so sorry, sir," said Dr. Zinchenko, still bracing herself against the banister on the second-floor balcony.

"As am I," said Mr. Lemoncello, his shoulders sagging. "As am I."

"You should be more than sorry!" shouted Mrs. Chiltington from the gallery. "You should be ashamed, Mr. Lemoncello. This is no way to run a library! Missing children's books *and* encyclopedias?"

"This is egregious!" shouted Charles.

"The people of Alexandriaville deserve better!" added his mother.

"This is also heinous!" said Charles. "And atrocious, too."

Mr. Lemoncello held up a shiny green medal. "I suppose I could cut this thing in two and award one half to each of you. But I might need a laser beam or a hacksaw. . . ."

"Why would you give Sierra anything?" demanded Marjory. "You asked for a date; I gave you a date. She gave you nothing except the name of a holiday."

"And a year," said Akimi. "Sierra got the year right, too."

Marjory snorted. "Too bad she couldn't come up with the month and day like I did. Then she'd actually have *a date*!"

"I suppose you are correct, Miss Muldauer," said Mr. Lemoncello. "Sound the jubilee; the Midwest team wins another medal."

"This isn't fair!" grumbled Miguel.

"There's still the twelfth game," said Kyle. "If we win it, we'll be all tied up again."

"And we can do that sudden-death overtime thing," said Akimi.

"Miss Muldauer?" said Mr. Lemoncello. "Please step forward and receive your prize."

Marjory strutted to the center of the room.

"For answering our most important questions most correctly, it is my honor to award you the most important medal of all the very important medals awarded thus far: the Yertle the Turtle."

"Huh?" said Marjory. "Why'd you give it a dumb name like that?"

"Because, Miss Muldauer, Dr. Seuss's book was considered extremely controversial when it first came out in 1958, for including the word 'burp.'" Mr. Lemoncello belched. "Sorry. Guzzled too much Lemonberry Fizz while I was recharging my batteries. *Yertle the Turtle* has also been banned because of its political messages."

"Whatever," said Marjory.

She snatched the medal out of Mr. Lemoncello's hand,

twirled around, and dangled her new prize in front of Team Kyle.

Kyle tried to ignore her. "What's the next game?" he asked Mr. Lemoncello.

Just then, a voice rang out behind Kyle.

"Stand aside, please. Coming through."

It was Clarence, the security guard, wading through the crowd of spectators.

"Mr. Lemoncello?" he said, waving a stack of papers. "You need to see this."

"What is it?"

"A list of all the titles currently missing from the library shelves. Dr. Zinchenko asked us to put one together after that last *Flora and Ulysses* book disappeared from the fiction wall."

"That looks like a mighty thick stack of paper, Clarence."

"Yes, sir. Ten pages."

"Any encyclopedias on your list?"

"Every single 'S' volume in the building."

Mr. Lemoncello shook his head and drooped in his seat.

"Enough. I'm done. I can't fight this fight alone anymore."

He slowly rose off his stool and gave his town-crier bell a weak jingle.

"Hear ye, hear ye. Oyez, oyez. The games of the first Library Olympiad are hereby suspended. If you have trouble understanding the word 'suspended,' kindly look it up in a dictionary, but forget checking an encyclopedia, because all the 'S' volumes have gone missing."

"Does this mean I win?" shouted Marjory.

"No, Miss Muldauer. It means I am tired of playing games here in Alexandriaville. Nobody wins. Everybody loses."

"What about those college scholarships you promised?" said one of the other members of the Midwest team.

Mr. Lemoncello turned to his head librarian.

"Dr. Zinchenko? Kindly give a 'Go to College Free' card to each and every Library Olympian."

She started passing out small orange cards.

"Tomorrow," said Mr. Lemoncello, "you shall all receive a full scholarship *if* you remember to bring that card with you to the closing ceremonies. If you should somehow lose it between now and then, I might pretend I don't know who you are, what you want, or what it was I promised to give you."

Dr. Zinchenko handed Kyle his "Go to College Free" card.

It was the size of a "Luck" or "Fortune" card from Mr. Lemoncello's Family Frenzy board game.

But this rectangle of flat cardboard was worth thousands and thousands of dollars.

Still, Kyle wished Mr. Lemoncello didn't look so sad. He wished he had drawn a "Find the Missing Books" card instead. He wished they could all go back to playing games.

When the thirty-two "Go to College Free" cards were handed out, Mr. Lemoncello narrowed his eyes and peered at the players.

"Hearty and splendiferous congratulations to you all," he said without any of his usual zip. "However, I have a sinking feeling that at least one of you doesn't really need a scholarship from me anymore."

42

Kyle watched the audience shuffle out of the building.

Most of the Library Olympians were thrilled to hear that they'd be picking up an all-expenses-paid college scholarship even without winning the most medals.

The Chiltingtons and their well-dressed friends were overjoyed for other reasons.

"Marvelous work, Miss Muldauer!" said Mrs. Chiltington when Marjory and her team passed by on their way to the front door. "Simply marvelous! You completely demoralized the man."

"Fantastic finish," added Charles. "Getting Lemoncello to cancel these so-called Olympic Games? Couldn't have done it in an abler manner myself."

"Mr. Lemoncello looked so sad," giggled Mrs. Chiltington. "I wouldn't be surprised if he packed up all his toys and went home to New York City!"

"If he does, it might be for the best," Marjory told her small cluster of fans. "For far too long, Mr. Lemoncello has pretended to be a library lover when, in truth, this was all a clever publicity stunt so he could sell even more of his preposterous games!"

The League of Concerned Library Lovers clapped daintily.

"Maybe now you concerned citizens, those of you who love libraries qua libraries, can run this institution the way we all know it should be run. If you turn this book-filled building into a true temple of learning, people all over Ohio will say, 'Is that library down in Alexandriaville any good?' To which you can reply, 'Hello? It's *not* a Lemoncello. It's a library!' "

Her admirers' hands pitter-pattered together again.

Marjory nodded graciously, then headed through the lobby with the rest of her team. Actually, the other kids from the Midwest team weren't really walking *with* Marjory, just in the same general direction.

"Where'd Mr. Lemoncello go?" asked Akimi.

"I saw him and Clarence head upstairs," said Sierra. "Probably to console Dr. Zinchenko."

"Definitely," said Miguel. "Librarians always flip out when books and encyclopedias mysteriously disappear off their shelves."

Mrs. Yunghans and Mr. Sharp, the hometown team's two chaperones, came to join the players at the reading desk.

"You guys ready to bookmobile it back to Olympia Village?" asked Mr. Sharp.

"Not just yet," said Kyle. "We want to make sure Mr. Lemoncello is okay."

"All right," said Mr. Sharp. "But it's barbecue night at the motel."

"We're not really in the mood for barbecue," said Akimi.

"They have ice cream, too," said Mrs. Yunghans.

Akimi crinkled her nose. "I think I'm suddenly lactose intolerant."

"We won't be long," said Kyle, tucking his orange scholarship card into his shirt pocket. "Come on, you guys."

As his team trooped up the spiral staircase to the second floor, Kyle looked down at the Rotunda Reading Room and realized how hollow the library seemed without anybody in it.

No one was riding the hover ladders or grabbing a snack in the Book Nook Café or hanging out in the community meeting rooms or rushing upstairs to do research at a collaboration station or heading to the third floor to check out the newest educational video games in the Electronic Learning Center.

The holographic statue nooks were empty and dark.

The Wonder Dome was just a blank canvas. A TV set after the power goes out.

Without people or laughter or learning, the domed building was just a fancy tomb filled with dry and dusty books.

43

"Mr. Lemoncello?" Kyle shouted, his voice echoing under the dome. "Dr. Zinchenko?"

"We are back here," replied Dr. Zinchenko. "Outside the zero-zero-zero door."

Kyle and his teammates made their way around the circular balcony.

Mr. Lemoncello, Dr. Zinchenko, and Clarence were standing in the same spot that had served as the starting line for the Library Cart Relay Race. They flipped through Clarence's thick stack of papers with serious expressions on their faces.

"Hey, Mr. Lemoncello," said Kyle.

Mr. Lemoncello raised his left hand to silence Kyle and continued frowning at the list of missing books.

"Are you telling us one individual removed all thirty-six copies of *Flora and Ulysses*?" asked Dr. Zinchenko.

"Thirty-five of them," said Clarence. "Somebody else grabbed the last copy off the fiction wall. But our main suspect checked out multiple copies of other titles, too. Tracking his records, we see he's been working on his personal book removal project for close to a month."

"Are the books overdue?"

"Not yet, Dr. Z," said Clarence. "He auto-renewed them all online. We can't be certain, but we think he's also the one who removed all those 'S' encyclopedias."

"This is actually old news," said Mr. Lemoncello. "You see, Clarence, Dr. Zinchenko—I've known all along who was behind this nonsense. And why. Stopping him and bringing back all the missing books was to be our final challenge in the Library Olympics. I've already been handing out clues left and right. But I don't think I can continue with that plan. If he and his associates can recruit a child—a Library Olympian, no less—or a group of children for their cause, what hope is there?"

"We'll help you, sir," said Kyle.

"Will you, Mr. Keeley? I've already given away the grand prize. Thirty-two of them, in fact. I can't give your team a *grander* prize or even a grand piano."

"That's okay. We just want to keep playing and prove we're really champions. Besides, I thought finding the missing books was supposed to be the twelfth game."

"It was. Another treasure hunt of sorts."

"So if we find the books, we'd win the twelfth medal."

"And then we could do a sudden-death overtime against Marjory Muldauer," added Akimi.

Mr. Lemoncello shook his head. "What if I told you that you might need Miss Muldauer to safely retrieve all the books?"

Akimi made her famous "gag me now" gesture.

"I know, I know," said Mr. Lemoncello. "It's impossible. Asking you and the other Library Olympians to work together for a higher, common purpose? Forget I even mentioned it. Dr. Zinchenko?"

"Sir?"

"I've made up my mind even though I have not yet made up my bed. I, Luigi Libretto Lemoncello, hereby officially declare the games of this first Library Olympiad to be over. Done. Kaput. There will be no winners. This library has failed to find its true champions. Tomorrow night, at the closing ceremonies, kindly hand out one college scholarship to each and every player who presents you with an orange card. I'm afraid I won't be able to attend the festivities. I'll be out of town. Either on a bridge to Terabithia or flying home to New York City. In fact, I may never return to Alexandriaville or Ohio again."

This was just about the worst news Kyle had ever heard.

"Mr. Lemoncello?" he said. "If you know who checked out all the books, why don't you tell the police and have the guy arrested?"

"The books are not yet overdue," said Dr. Zinchenko.

"And, if I might cite the American Library Association's code of ethics . . ."

"Please, Dr. Z, cite away," said Mr. Lemoncello.

"Here at the Lemoncello Library, we protect each library user's right to privacy and confidentiality with respect to information sought or received and resources consulted, borrowed, acquired, or transmitted."

"Seriously?" said Akimi.

"Oh, yeah," said Miguel. "It's the library law."

Kyle tried one more time. "But, Mr. Lemoncello . . ."

His hero raised that hand again.

"It was fun, Mr. Keeley, but now we're done. Dr. Zinchenko? Monday morning, kindly instruct my lawyers to draw up the necessary papers appointing Mrs. Chiltington and her League of Concerned Library Lovers as the Alexandriaville Public Library's first board of trustees. Then take down my statue and pack up anything with my name on it, including my last case of Mr. Lemoncello's Lemonberry Fizz."

"But what if we find the missing books?" Kyle pleaded.

"I told you—I'm through handing out medals. There are no more prizes, Kyle. No more ice cream, cake, or balloons."

"I don't care." Kyle turned to his teammates. "How about you guys?"

They all shook their heads.

"Nope," said Miguel.

"The medals clash with my earrings," added Akimi.

"Fine," said Mr. Lemoncello. "Suit yourself. Play my final game, find the missing books before tomorrow's closing ceremonies, and I might—I repeat, *might*—reconsider turning my library over to Mrs. Chiltington. I might also consider staying in Ohio on a permanent basis."

"Thank you, sir," said Kyle. "Because we don't really need to win any more medals or scholarships. But we definitely need you. And our library."

44

Around midnight, after celebrating the defeat of Mr. Lemoncello with Charles and Marjory over a few bottles of root beer, Andrew Peckleman still needed to sweep up around the motel.

Even though it was very late, he heard voices coming from his uncle's office, so he worked his broom and dustpan closer to the door.

He heard his uncle Woody, Marjory Muldauer . . .

. . . and Mrs. Chiltington?

Andrew pressed his back against the wall and listened.

His uncle was chuckling. "Luigi is really leaving town?"

"So it would seem," said Mrs. Chiltington. "I just received a call from that Russian woman, Dr. Zinfluenzo. She suggested that I come by the library first thing Monday morning. Apparently, Mr. Lemoncello's lawyers are drawing up papers to transfer the stewardship of 'his' library to its new board of trustees."

"That's you and your friends, right?" said Marjory.

"Yes. The League of Concerned Library Lovers will make certain that the new Alexandriaville Public Library undertakes a major course correction and no longer subjects children to corrupting influences and mindless frivolity."

"And to think," said his uncle, "Luigi's unraveling really started with one book. The one you plucked off the shelf for me, Marjory. It was the straw that broke the camel's back."

"How did you know losing *Flora and Ulysses* would have that effect on him, Mr. Peckleman?" asked Marjory.

The old man cackled. "Because Luigi's smart. He figured out that one of you library-loving kids was helping me hoard every single copy of that terrible book. It broke his heart. Crushed his spirit."

"Well . . ."

Andrew could hear a slight quaver in Marjory's voice. She took a deep breath.

"I'm very glad I could help you two save a library from turning into a cheap, Floo-powdered World of Wizardry tourist trap," she continued, her voice shaky. "However, now that Mr. Lemoncello is relinquishing control, we should take back that book I borrowed. Maybe I can drop it off in the sidewalk book-return slot when no one is watching."

208

"No need for us to do that, dear," said Andrew's uncle.

"I disagree," said Marjory. "I can't just walk back into the library with the book."

"Of course not. What I meant to say is there is absolutely no need for us to *ever* take back a single copy of that particular book. The library has plenty of other books. No one will miss one more."

"It's true," said Mrs. Chiltington. "There are so many wonderful children's books. I have suggestions for others we should stock, as well."

"But *Flora and Ulysses* won the Newbery Medal," said Marjory. "There should always be at least one copy on the shelves in any library."

"Perhaps," said Mrs. Chiltington. "Perhaps not. It seems rather childish to me."

"It's a children's book. It's meant to be childish."

"Miss Muldauer," said Mrs. Chiltington, "I'm sure our new librarians will give your concerns about this *Flora and Ulysses* the attention they deserve. However, since you live in Michigan and not here in Ohio, you may not be fully aware of our local tastes and opinions about which books do and do not belong on our library shelves."

"Besides," said Andrew's uncle, "I don't like that book. It's one of the worst of its kind."

"There are other books that *I* don't like," added Mrs. Chiltington. "For instance, that *Yertle the Turtle*. It is rather subversive. Not at all what our children need to be reading if we expect them to grow up properly. There are also some local history books that are quite biased in their interpretation of the past. One entitled *Ohio River Pirates and Scallywags,* for instance, is full of lies, innuendo, and misinformation. It should, once again, be pulled from the shelves."

"B-b-but . . . ," stammered Marjory.

"Thank you, Miss Muldauer, for all your help. Thanks to you, our lovely new library shall soon become a true library. With none of Mr. Lemoncello's lunacy."

Andrew quickly swept away from the door.

He couldn't believe his ears.

His great-uncle-twice-removed and Mrs. Chiltington were trying to ban certain books from the Alexandriaville Public Library.

Books they didn't like.

The two of them were nearly as bad as all those book burners and banners Andrew used to hate back when he loved libraries.

Which, actually, he still kind of did.

First thing in the morning, the bookmobile dropped off Kyle and his teammates in front of the library.

"I'll wait here," said the driver.

"Thanks," said Kyle.

He and his teammates bustled up the front steps and entered the library.

The statue of Mr. Lemoncello was gone.

Someone had slathered wet cement over the "Knowledge Not Shared Remains Unknown" motto chiseled into the fountain's base.

"Mr. Lemoncello has left the building," said Clarence, coming out of the control room off the lobby.

"We can see that," said Kyle. "Somebody took out the statue."

"Mr. Lemoncello," said Clarence. "He wanted to ship it back to his factory in New Jersey. They have a garden."

211

"Who erased his slogan?" asked Sierra.

"The new board of trustees. They don't officially take over till sometime Monday, but they've already started making changes. They have a new slogan: 'Shush!' Now they're inside, trying to figure out how to dismantle the hover ladders."

"Oh, no they're not," said Kyle. "The hover ladders are awesome!"

Kyle stormed into the Rotunda Reading Room with Miguel, Akimi, and Sierra right behind him.

Charles Chiltington was jabbing at one of the hover ladder bases with a pointy-tipped screwdriver.

"Knock it off, Charles," said Kyle.

"Oh, hello, Keeley. What are you doing here in mother's library?"

"It's not her library," said Akimi.

"Well, it will be soon enough," said Charles. "When I'm finished grounding these ridiculous contraptions, I'll be heading upstairs with my wire cutters. Mummy wants me to snip the power cables to all those senseless video games."

"That is so *not* going to happen," said Miguel.

"Really? Who's going to stop me?"

"I will!" said the holographic librarian, Lonni Gause. She didn't seem to be flickering as much as she usually did.

"What?" laughed Charles. "I don't mean to be rude, lady, but you're not real."

"That's right. I'm a virtual librarian. That means I live up in the cloud inside a computer—a computer connected to the four hundred and ninety-eight different security cameras currently operational inside this library. I'm also linked to the Web and know exactly how to send streaming video footage of you vandalizing that expensive equipment to the local and state police. It's amazing what you can do when you share knowledge with others."

"You wouldn't dare. My mother is—"

"Just another library card holder until Monday."

"The make-believe librarian is correct, Charles," said Mrs. Chiltington as she came out of the Book Nook Café, sipping a cup of tea with her pinky finger extended.

"I should've known," gasped Mrs. Gause. "It's you again!"

Mrs. Chiltington smiled and sipped her tea.

"Yo," said Miguel. "No food or beverages are allowed in the library. You have to drink that in the Book Nook Café or dump it down the sink."

Clarence and Clement strode into the Rotunda Reading Room.

"Somebody sipping tea where they shouldn't be sipping it?" asked Clarence.

"Yes," said the holographic librarian. "Kindly escort Mrs. Chiltington and her disruptive son out of the building. And whatever you do, don't let that woman anywhere near the nine hundreds room!"

"There's no need for an escort," huffed Mrs. Chiltington. "We know the way out. Come along, Charles dear. But, Mrs. Gause?"

"Yes?"

"First thing Monday morning, I'm personally pulling your plug."

As soon as the Chiltingtons were gone, Kyle turned to Mrs. Gause.

"We want to play the final game."

"The book quest?"

"Yes, ma'am. We figured that if it was supposed to be the twelfth game, like Mr. Lemoncello said it was, there might be some clues to start us off."

"I'm not aware of any new clues. Just the ones he's already handed out."

"What about those security cameras that caught Charles?" asked Kyle. "Did they record who took the last *Flora and Ulysses* off the shelf? Mr. Lemoncello said it had to be one of the Olympians. Maybe one of the losing teams did it so nobody else could win."

"Um, Kyle?" said Akimi. "How would they know what book to take?"

"I don't know. Maybe they hacked into Dr. Zinchenko's computer."

Akimi arched an eyebrow. "You're making this up as you go, right?"

"Yeah."

"Unfortunately," said Mrs. Gause, "all the fiction wall

cameras were not functioning from the start of the Library Olympics until ten minutes ago."

"Look, Mrs. Gause," said Kyle, "we need to find those missing books. Before tonight."

"And we want you to find them," said Mrs. Gause.

"Indeed we do," said one of the holographic statues, which had just appeared under the Wonder Dome. Benjamin Franklin.

Now all the other nook statues came to illuminated life and started shouting. "Save this library!" "You can do it, lads and lasses!" "Your library is your paradise!"

"It's all the famous librarians again," said Miguel.

"The task you four are attempting is very difficult," said Mrs. Gause. "It's also extremely complex. It might take you *and* all of the other teams to unravel this particular puzzle."

"Everybody's still at the motel," said Akimi, "because Dr. Z is handing out those scholarships tonight at the closing ceremonies."

"Well," said Mrs. Gause, "you don't really need *all* of them. Just the winners. The ones who received medals?" Then she winked. Several times.

"The medals!" said Kyle. "Of course. All those goofy names. They're clues. Mr. Lemoncello said he'd been handing clues out right and left. He's been setting us up for this final game since the first day of the Library Olympics."

Suddenly, the Wonder Dome was filled with an "instant

replay" video collage of Mr. Lemoncello handing out eleven different medals.

"So," said Miguel, "anybody remember what all those different medals were called?"

"Sorry," said Sierra. "I guess we should've taken notes."

"Come on, you guys," said Kyle. "We're going back to Olympia Village. We have some medals to inspect."

46

"What are we going to learn from all the medals?" asked Sierra as the bookmobile raced back to Olympia Village.

"I don't know," said Kyle.

"Maybe there's something etched on the back," suggested Miguel. "Maybe parts of a map, like in that movie *National Treasure*. And if you arrange all the medals correctly, it'll make a treasure map that will lead us to the secret hiding place for the missing books!"

"Seriously?" said Akimi.

"Hey," said Kyle. "It's a possibility. We have to consider every angle."

"Even the screwy ones?"

"Yo," said Miguel, "we're talking about Luigi Lemoncello. Screwy is usually his first choice."

"Do you think Marjory Muldauer is going to let us even look at the four medals she won?" asked Sierra.

"No way," said Akimi. "If she finds out we're trying to win the twelfth game, even though there isn't any prize . . ."

"Except saving Mr. Lemoncello's library," said Kyle.

"A library that, by the way, Marjory Muldauer despises," added Miguel.

"My point exactly," said Akimi. "She isn't going to play along with us, Kyle."

"Well, we have to try. Mr. Lemoncello said we might need Marjory to 'win' this round. Not that we're actually going to *win* anything."

When they reached Olympia Village, most of the other teams were hanging out in the dining area, scarfing down bacon and playing with the waffle machines.

"Um, you guys," said Kyle, standing near the fireplace at one end of the room, "don't mean to interrupt your breakfasts, but we sort of need your help."

"What for?" asked Elliott Schilpp, the kid from Maryland, who seemed to enjoy bacon as much as he enjoyed pizza.

"Someone has been taking books out of the Lemoncello Library," said Akimi, "and not bringing them back."

"Finding the missing books was supposed to be the twelfth game in the Library Olympics," explained Kyle.

"So do we win an extra prize if we help you folks figure this thing out?" asked Angus Harper from Texas.

"Not really," said Akimi. "Neither will we. Mr.

Lemoncello's basically canceled the whole Library Olympics dealio."

"But we need to find them anyway," said Kyle. "Otherwise, Mr. Lemoncello is going to leave town and his awesomely incredible library will get turned into Mrs. Borington's Snoozeville Book Depository."

"They'll bring in old-fashioned librarians to shush people," added Miguel.

"Well, if we don't win anything extra by helping you guys," groused the guy from New York City, "why should we help? We've already scored our college scholarships."

"Actually," said Kyle, "you *will* win something else if you help us do this thing."

"Yeah? What?"

"You'll all get to come back to Alexandriaville as often as you like and have fun doing research or learning junk about flying prehistoric reptiles or talking to famous holograms, like this amazing rocket scientist we met, or just reading a good book you found while you were floating along and browsing the fiction wall in Mr. Lemoncello's amazingly incredible library."

The whole room was quiet. There wasn't even a fork clink or a milk slurp.

Finally, Angus stood up. "Sounds good to me."

Stephanie Youngerman from the Mountain team was on her feet next. "What do you guys need?"

"Ah, what the hey," said the kid from New York. "Sign me up."

"Me too!" said Elliott Schilpp, his mouth full of bacon.

"Thanks, you guys," said Kyle. "First we need to see everybody's medals. Including the ones the Midwest team won."

"Oh, you mean the ones Marjory Muldauer said she won all by herself?" said a girl in a Wisconsin Badgers baseball cap.

"Don't worry," said Margaret Miles, a chaperone for the Midwest team. "I made Marjory turn them over to me."

"Is Marjory around?" asked Kyle.

"She went for a walk with our other chaperone," said Ms. Miles. "Father Mike from Regis Catholic Middle School in Cedar Rapids, Iowa. They should be back soon."

That's when Andrew Peckleman stepped into the dining room.

"Kyle?" he said. "We need to talk."

47

"We're kind of in the middle of something, Andrew," Kyle said politely.

Andrew put his hand alongside his mouth and whispered, "I know who grabbed that last copy of *Flora and Ulysses*."

Kyle motioned for Andrew to step out of the room with him.

"First off," said Kyle, "I'm really sorry about that garbage man crack I made the other day."

"You were under a lot of pressure. I know how that feels. When we played the escape game, Charles Chiltington put so much pressure on me I thought I might turn into a diamond."

Kyle must've looked confused.

"You know," said Andrew. "The way Superman can squeeze a lump of coal so hard that it turns into a diamond?"

"Riiight," said Kyle. "So, who swiped the book off the shelf?"

Andrew took a moment. "Marjory Muldauer. That's why she's with the priest. I think she feels bad and is giving him her full confession!"

"But why would she take the book?"

"Because my uncle Woody told her to."

Is that why Mr. Peckleman offered cheat cards to Miguel and Sierra? Kyle wondered. *Maybe he wasn't working for Mr. Lemoncello but against him!*

"Late last night," said Andrew, "I heard them both talking with Mrs. Chiltington about taking the book off the shelf. Uncle Woody had already checked out the other thirty-five copies, and he probably would've checked out the last one, too, except regular people weren't allowed in the library for a whole week while they fixed up the place for the Olympics."

Now Kyle wondered if this was why Marjory had blocked him instead of going for the book during the hover ladder race.

She had known the last copy of *Flora and Ulysses* wouldn't be on the shelf, because she'd already removed it. She probably didn't think she was a good enough actress to be the one who found the empty slot. But she didn't want Kyle finding it, either, because she assumed Mr. Lemoncello would give a medal to whoever found the spot where the book was supposed to be.

"Okay. So why did your uncle want the last copy of *Flora and Ulysses*?"

"I'm not sure," said Andrew. "But I am formulating a theory. It has to do with all those other books and encyclopedias you guys say are missing from the library. Do you have a complete list?"

Kyle shook his head. He should've thought of that.

How were they going to return all the missing books if they didn't even know what books were missing?

Then it hit him.

"Clarence does!"

"Who?"

"The head of security. Come on."

Kyle and Andrew went back into the dining area.

"You guys?" said Kyle.

"What's up?" asked Akimi.

"Andrew and I need to head back downtown. Sierra? Can you come with us?"

Sierra looked at Andrew, the boy who had stolen her library card during the escape game.

"I never really wanted to steal your library card," said Andrew. "Honestly. Charles made me do it."

"I know," said Sierra. Then she took a deep breath. "Should I tell the driver to fire up the bookmobile?"

"Definitely," said Kyle. "Go with Sierra, Andrew. I'll meet you guys out front."

"What's up?" asked Miguel.

"We have a lead on who might've checked out all those books."

"So what do you need the rest of us to do while you guys are gone?" asked Akimi.

"Round up all the medals. Make a list. See if there is some kind of pattern or hidden code."

"Or a treasure map etched on their backs!" said Miguel.

"Riiight. Or that. You guys have your phones?"

"Totally," said Akimi.

"Cool. Whoever finds out something first—"

"Calls the other ones."

Clarence met Kyle, Sierra, and Andrew in the lobby.

"We're looking for the missing books," said Kyle.

"Well, not to bust your chops, Mr. Keeley," said Clarence, "but I think you're looking in the wrong place. The books aren't here in the library. If they were, they wouldn't be missing."

"We know," said Kyle. "But we need to see your list."

"Why?"

"I have a theory," said Andrew.

Clarence gestured for the three treasure hunters to follow him through the red door into the control room.

"Here's the list. Hope it helps. I'll be out in the lobby if you need anything else."

Clarence left. Andrew and Sierra studied the pages.

"Aha!" said Andrew. "I was right."

"Good going, Andrew," said Sierra. "It's so obvious."

Kyle looked down at the list.

He had no idea what they were talking about.

48

"Have you read *Flora and Ulysses*?" Andrew asked Kyle.

Kyle looked at the floor and sort of shuffled his feet. "I wanted to. But all the copies were checked out or missing and . . ."

"It's about a squirrel, Kyle," said Sierra with a smile.

"So are all these other books," said Andrew.

Sierra read a few titles off the list. "*The Tale of Squirrel Nutkin* by Beatrix Potter. *The Bravest Squirrel Ever* by Sara Shafer. *Earl the Squirrel* by Don Freeman."

"*Earl*'s a great audiobook, too," said Andrew. "Uncle Woody also checked out every single book from the five hundreds room about squirrels—all three subcategories under 599.36 for Sciuridae."

"For *who*?" said Kyle.

" 'Sciuridae' means 'squirrel family,' " explained Sierra.

"Indeed it does," said Andrew, smiling at Sierra, who, believe it or not, was smiling back at him. "Uncle Woody took everything Mr. Lemoncello had about tree squirrels, ground squirrels, *and* flying squirrels."

"And then," said Sierra, "he went downstairs and scooped up all the Rocky and Bullwinkle DVDs."

"Because Rocky is a flying squirrel!" added Andrew eagerly. "He also removed all the 'S' encyclopedias. . . ."

"Because they'd have squirrels in them," said Kyle, finally catching on. "But why does your uncle need all these books? Is he some kind of squirrel nut?"

Andrew laughed. "Touché, Kyle. Very clever."

Sierra laughed, too. "I get it. Squirrel—nut."

"And Uncle Woody was *squirreling* away all the squirrel books he could!"

"So," said Kyle, "for whatever reason, your uncle loves squirrels so much he has to hoard every single squirrel book he can find?"

"Oh, no," said Andrew, sounding deadly serious again. He adjusted his glasses with his fingertip. "My uncle doesn't love squirrels. He *hates* them. What he loves are birds."

"Right," said Kyle. "All those bird feeders on the motel property. Calling it the Blue Jay Extended Stay Lodge. The way he looked at those birds up on the Wonder Dome that day."

"Correct. Uncle Woody thinks squirrels are 'nothing but thieving rodents' and 'rats with fluffy tails.' They make a mess of all his bird feeders."

"So since he hates squirrels, he doesn't want anybody else reading about them?"

Andrew shrugged. "I guess. Like we said, he's kind of nutty."

Kyle snapped his fingers. "This is why that Squirrel Squad video game never worked in the motel game room."

"Uncle Woody probably snipped the power cord."

"Do you know where he put the books?" asked Kyle.

"No," said Andrew. "I only started figuring this out early this morning, after I heard Uncle Woody talking to Marjory about *Flora and Ulysses*. However, if you guys will have me, I'd like to help you find the missing books."

"You would?"

"Certainly. No matter how much I disagree with Mr. Lemoncello and his loony ideas about libraries, I totally respect his right to stock his shelves with whatever books he chooses—and our right to read them."

Sierra was beaming when Andrew said that.

Kyle's phone started chirping. It was Akimi.

"What've you got?" he asked her.

"Meet us in Liberty Park, across the street from the motel."

"We're on our way." He ended the call. "Come on, you guys!"

"Where are we going?" asked Andrew.

"Liberty Park."

"Why?"

"I have no idea."

Kyle, Sierra, and Andrew piled into the bookmobile and took off.

"The park is right across the street from my uncle's motel," said Andrew. "Maybe he buried the squirrel books in the sandbox or something."

"All of them?" asked Sierra.

"Hang on, you guys," said Kyle as he thumb-dialed Akimi.

"Where are you, Kyle?" said Akimi the instant she answered.

"On our way."

"Well, hurry. We're all kind of confused."

"Who's with you?"

"Miguel and one player from each of the other teams."

"Nice. Whose idea was that?"

"Mine."

"Sweet!"

"Yeah. I can be very diplomatic when I'm about to lose my favorite library in the whole world."

"So what's up with Liberty Park? What sent you there?"

"The medals!" said Akimi. "Stephanie Youngerman from the Mountain team is an excellent code cracker. She's the one who figured it out."

"Figured what out?"

"Okay, here's the list of medals in the order they were given out: Gold, Olympian, Top Gun—"

"We won that one."

"We also won the Olympian Researcher. After that, Marjory scored the Libris. Then came the 'I Did It!,' the Bendable Bookworm, Eating It Up, Rebus, Thank You, and Yertle the Turtle medallions."

"Are they anagrams or something?"

"Nope. It's another version of Mr. Lemoncello's First Letters game. When you write down the first letter of all eleven medals, guess what it says."

Kyle had already scribbled out the answer on a scrap of paper: "Go to Liberty."

"Exactly," said Akimi. "And you said Mr. Lemoncello never repeats himself, never uses the same kind of clue twice."

"Well, he didn't. Not the exact same way."

"Whatever. But now that we're over here at the park, we don't know what we're looking for."

"Books about squirrels."

"Wha-hut?"

"That's what Andrew Peckleman figured out. His uncle Woody hates squirrels, on account of all his bird feeders. So he doesn't want anybody else in town reading about them, either."

"Why? Does he think that if all the squirrel books disappear, the squirrels will disappear, too?"

"Maybe."

"The man is definitely nutty," said Akimi.

Three minutes later, the bookmobile squealed to a stop outside Liberty Park, which was actually more of a playground with trees and picnic tables.

"You guys find anything?" Kyle asked Miguel.

"No. No signs of digging."

"Why are you looking for signs of digging?"

"Buried treasure, man. Like in *Treasure Island*."

"I don't think Mr. Peckleman would've buried his books over here," said the Texan, Angus Harper. "Somebody would've seen him doing it."

"You're right," said Kyle. "He wouldn't take that big of a risk."

"So why did Mr. Lemoncello send us here?" asked Diane Capriola, from the Southeast team.

"Liberty Park!" said Stephanie Youngerman. "It's another anagram!"

Everybody whipped out their smartphones and started using the notes app to rearrange the letters.

"Perky tribal!" shouted Miguel.

"Library kept!" said Stephanie Youngerman. "It has 'library' in it!"

While the other treasure hunters kept calling out weird word combinations, Kyle slowly rotated in place, scanning the park and the playground.

"What's that?" He pointed to a green humped structure with a bobble head attached to one side by a stubby neck made of coiled spring.

"That's for kids to climb on," said Andrew. "It's supposed to look like a turtle."

"And," said Kyle, "when Mr. Lemoncello gave Marjory Muldauer her Yertle the Turtle medal, he said it was the 'most important medal of all the very important medals awarded thus far.' Come on."

Kyle led the way to the shell-shaped turtle toy. Pranav Pillai, from the Pacific team, scooted under it.

"Score!" he shouted.

"What'd you find?" asked Kyle.

Pranav slid out from under the turtle and showed everybody what he'd found: a bright yellow envelope with "Clue" stamped on its front.

Kyle looked at what was written on the yellow card tucked into the yellow envelope:

41.376495
−83.651040

"Guess we better head back to the library," he said with a sigh. "More Dewey decimal numbers."

"Whoa, hang on," said Miguel.

"Those are not Dewey numbers, my friend," said Pranav Pillai.

"There aren't any negative numbers in Mr. Dewey's library classification system," explained Elliott Schilpp.

"I believe Mr. Lemoncello is inviting us to play a geocaching game," said Angus Harper. "Because those numbers sure look like GPS coordinates to me."

"What's geocaching?" asked Sierra.

"An outdoor recreational activity," said Pranav Pillai, "where one uses a GPS device and other navigational techniques to hide and seek waterproof containers that each have a logbook sealed inside, where you can sign your name to indicate that you found it."

Kyle smiled. A lot of these library experts sounded like dictionaries.

Angus Harper pulled out his smartphone. "And it just so happens that I have a GPS navigation app on my phone. Most fliers do. We tap in longitude 41.376495 and latitude negative 83.651040 and—*BOOM!*—this map shows us where to go."

A red pin dropped on the app's map, indicating a spot just across the street from Liberty Park.

"That's near the motel!" said Miguel.

"Looks like the mailbox out front!" said Andrew.

"Let's go check it out," said Kyle.

The group of twelve new teammates trooped down to the crosswalk, where they waited for the light to change.

"You can't miss the mailbox," said Andrew. "It's shaped like a bird."

The light changed.

Kyle and Akimi led the charge across the street to the boxy blue mailbox. It had wooden wings nailed to its sides and a tail feather on its rear. To open the drop-down front, you had to tug on the bluebird's beak.

"Another envelope," said Abia Sulayman when Kyle opened the mailbox.

"Is it official USPS mail?" asked Stephanie Younger-man. "If so, it is a federal offense for us to open it."

"No," said Kyle. "It's another yellow envelope with 'Clue' stamped on the front."

"Open it," urged Angus.

Kyle tore open the envelope.

"It's a bunch of riddles," he reported. "Three of them."

Diane Capriola, who had won her spot on the South-east team by solving riddles, stepped forward.

"Let me see that," she said.

Kyle was pretty good with riddles, too, but he handed the envelope over to Diane.

"First riddle," she said. " 'What has four wheels and flies?' "

"An airplane!" blurted Miguel.

"Hold that thought," said Diane. "Second riddle: 'You'll find your next clue in the red stump.' "

The other eleven kids started looking around the motel grounds, searching for a brightly painted tree stump.

"And finally, riddle three: 'Everything I do goes to waste.' " She closed up the envelope. "All three clues are sending us to the same place."

"The woods?" said Nicole Wisniewski, who was still looking for the red stump. "I'm not big on woods. I'm from Chicago."

"No," said Diane. "The third riddle is a pun. The second riddle is a jumble. And the first riddle is for kindergartners."

"So, Kyle," said Akimi, "that means you can probably handle it."

Kyle grinned. "That's okay. I'm sure Diane knows the answer."

"Yep," she said. "The Dumpster."

"This way," said Andrew. "It's behind the kitchen."

He led the way around the main building to a small loading dock in the back.

"Oh, I get it," said Miguel. "The Dumpster has four wheels and attracts flies."

"Also," said Sierra, " 'Dumpster' and 'red stump' are spelled with the same letters."

"Yep," said Diane, "and everything a Dumpster does 'goes to waste.' "

"Good work," said Kyle. "Now who wants to lift the lid?"

Even closed, the Dumpster reeked of rotting fruit and rancid dairy products.

"You," said Akimi, pointing at Kyle with one hand while swatting at the foul air and buzzing flies with the other. "You're the team captain."

"Of our hometown team," said Kyle, "but not this one. This is more like one of those superhero teams in the comic books."

"We could be the Justice League of Libraries," said Pranav Pillai eagerly.

236

The guy sounded like he *really* liked comic books.

"All in favor of Kyle Keeley being our captain, no matter what our team is called, please raise your right hand," said Akimi.

Everybody, including Andrew Peckleman, shot one hand into the air. They were using their other hands to hold their noses or fan the air in front of their faces.

The vote was unanimous.

Kyle was elected captain. He would open the Dumpster.

He might also need to climb inside it.

51

Even though he was lifting a lid on a fly factory, Kyle was feeling pretty pumped.

This new team of super library geeks seemed invincible. They were Mr. Lemoncello's Champion Crusaders, standing up for what was right in a world gone wrong. Sharing knowledge to boldly conquer the unknown.

Or something like that.

Kyle watched a lot of movie trailers.

A warm blast of sour-milk-rotten-lettuce-dirty-diaper air made Kyle's eyes water as he raised the rubbery lid on the Dumpster.

Fortunately, a plastic-wrapped envelope labeled "Clue," with something rectangular in it, was attached to the lid's underside. There would be no need for Dumpster diving.

Kyle tugged the envelope free and heard the unmistakable sound of Velcro strips separating. He tossed the package, which felt like a wrapped-up book, to Andrew. Kyle let go of the lid and the Dumpster's rubber cover slammed.

"Can we go somewhere a little less rank to open it?" asked Akimi, trying to breathe only through her mouth.

"Definitely," said Kyle.

The whole team scurried away from the loading dock and back to the parking lot outside the motel lobby.

"Where's your boss?" Akimi asked Andrew.

"He must be running errands. His truck is gone."

"Open it," Kyle said to Andrew.

Andrew tore at the tape and plastic bag protecting the thick yellow envelope with "Clue" inked on the front. Inside, he found a book.

He read the title out loud: " '*Louie the Locksmith's Big Book of Padlocks, Dead Bolts, and Tumblers*'?"

Pranav Pillai smiled at the book. "And so, old friend, we meet again."

"What do you mean?" asked Akimi.

"To earn my place on the Pacific team," said Pranav, "I had to use the Dewey decimal code on this very book."

He flipped the book sideways and read its spine.

"Oh, my. This is incorrect."

"I'll say," said Abia Sulayman. "It should be in the six hundreds with books about technology, not the nine hundreds with history and geography."

"What's the call number?" asked Andrew.

Pranav read it off: "Nine-four-three-point-seven."

"That is soooo wrong," said Andrew.

"True," said Pranav. "But it could be wrong on purpose. You see, when I played the escape game in Silicon Valley, the Dewey decimal number for the locksmith book was also the combination for the lock on the library door."

"So whatever lock we're looking for," said Sierra, "couldn't have the same combination as that one."

Andrew slapped his hand to his forehead, nearly smashing his goggle-sized glasses.

"The storage locker! I'm sorry, you guys. I should've thought of this sooner."

"That's okay, Andrew," said Sierra. "You thought of it now. Go on."

"Well, my uncle Woody has this humongous safe. The vault door is the size of a motel room door. It's hidden behind a sliding panel in the front office."

"Then this is most likely the combination," said Pranav.

"The office looks empty," reported Nicole Wisniewski, peering through the windows. "We should go check it out."

"All of us?" asked Elliott Schilpp.

"Yep," said Kyle. "There's strength in numbers."

"Kyle's right," said Akimi. "If Andrew's creepy uncle . . . No offense, Andrew. . . ."

Andrew held up his hand. "None taken."

Akimi continued: "If the birdman of Alexandriaville comes back, a dozen kids should be able to hold him at bay."

"We could tell him we just spotted an ivory-billed woodpecker or a blue-throated hummingbird," said Abia Sulayman.

"Huh?" said Akimi.

"Both species are very high on every birdwatcher's 'must see' list. I am something of a birder myself."

"Come on," said Kyle. "Let's go crack open that safe."

The twelve treasure hunters made their way through the lobby and into the motel office.

"That's the wall," said Andrew, pointing to the sheet of paneling sporting a framed portrait of two bluebirds.

"Which way does it slide?" asked Kyle.

"To the right," said Andrew.

He and Kyle put their hands on the wall and shoved it sideways.

The panel rolled away and revealed a tall steel door with a combination lock right above a thick metal handle.

"Okay, Pranav," said Kyle, "you're on."

Pranav Pillai stepped forward and spun the dial three times to clear it. Then he worked the combination.

"Right to nine. Left to four. Right to three. Left to seven."

He pressed down on the handle.

It didn't budge.

"Try it again," suggested Kyle. "But reverse it."

"Ah, yes," said Pranav. "An excellent suggestion."

He spun the dial to clear it, then worked the new combination.

"*Left* to nine. *Right* to four. Left to three. Right to seven."

Something clicked.

Pranav pressed down on the handle.

The door to the vault swung open.

The motel safe was huge, the size of a whole room, which was what it probably had been until Mr. Peckleman converted it into a steel-walled high-security vault.

It was also empty except for a couple of stacks of birdseed sacks. Kyle couldn't believe it.

"There's nothing in here," he said.

"But it looks like there used to be," said Angus Harper. "Check out those marks on the carpet." He pointed to the floor.

"Indentations that might've been made by heavy boxes," said Elliott Schilpp.

"Book boxes," added Sierra.

"No!" somebody screamed outside the motel. "You can't do it!"

"That sounds like Marjory," said Nicole Wisniewski. "She screamed at us all the time."

243

"Come on!" said Kyle.

The twelve treasure hunters tore out of the office, raced across the lobby, and headed out to the patio, where all the other Library Olympians and their chaperones were standing in a circle, staring at something that was making their jaws drop.

Kyle heard a crackle and a pop.

He pushed his way through the crowd.

Mr. Peckleman stood next to the blazing fire pit, laughing hysterically.

Marjory was there, too. Tears streamed down her cheeks.

"I'm begging you, sir," Marjory said. "Don't do this."

"What's going on?" demanded one of the chaperones.

"We're going to get rid of these wretched squirrel books, once and for all," cackled Mr. Peckleman.

"Oh, no you are not," said Akimi, shoving her way to the front of the crowd to join Kyle near the roaring fire pit.

Kyle could see garden carts, a little red wagon, and a wheelbarrow loaded down with books. On top of the pile closest to him was *Flora and Ulysses*.

"Marjory told me all about how you tricked her into stealing that book," said a man in a priest collar, who Kyle figured had to be Father Mike, chaperone for the Midwest team. "I'm going to call the police."

"Try it, Padre," snapped Mr. Peckleman, "and I start tossing books on the bonfire the second your finger touches your phone. I figure I can burn through most of 'em before the police even show up. They're very busy this afternoon down at the Lemoncello Library. It seems an anonymous tipster just phoned in a report of a major book burglary."

"That was you!" whined Andrew. "How can you do this, Uncle Woody?"

"Easy. You see, I agree with that lunatic Lemoncello: 'Knowledge not shared remains unknown.' Well, if I destroy this so-called knowledge about squirrels, no one will ever know it existed." He held up a copy of *Flora and Ulysses*. "A squirrel who writes poetry? *Pah!* Squirrels are nothing but thieving rodents. Rats with fluffy tails! They're bullies who steal food from innocent birds."

"Look, Mr. Peckleman," said Kyle, "just because you don't like books about squirrels . . ."

"Nobody else should, either! Don't you see, Mr. Keeley? I'm trying to protect you children. You shouldn't be forced to read lies about a squirrel named Earl who wears a red scarf and can't find his own acorn. Your young eyes should not be exposed to videos about a flying squirrel who shares his home with a talking moose."

"That's a cartoon," said Kyle. "It's not real."

Kyle didn't know what to do.

Mr. Peckleman was nuttier than any of them had suspected.

And the fire pit was really blazing.

If the police were busy downtown at the library, investigating the theft of the missing books, it would take them maybe ten minutes to race all the way up to the motel.

Mr. Peckleman could burn a ton of books in ten minutes.

Kyle had to do something. Saving Mr. Lemoncello's library had to include protecting its books, even the ones some people didn't like.

"Look, Mr. Peckleman, let's make a deal. . . ."

"Oh, that's right. Andrew told me about you. You're the game boy. You think you can make some kind of trade with me like you would if we were playing Monopoly?"

"Why not? What are you afraid of?"

"Not you, Kyle Keeley. Or any of your friends. What I am doing is right!"

"Then let's play a game. If we win, you don't burn a single book."

"And if *I* win?"

Kyle looked to Akimi.

She nodded.

He turned to Mrs. Yunghans.

"Do what you have to do, Kyle. We're running out of time."

Finally, Kyle looked at Marjory Muldauer.

She nodded, too.

"Okay, Mr. Peckleman," said Kyle, "if you can beat us in a game—"

The old man jabbed a finger at Kyle. "I get to choose the game, right?"

"Fine. But remember—if we win, you have to leave the books alone."

246

"Yes, I heard you the first time," said Mr. Peckleman. "But what do I get if I win?"

Kyle swallowed hard. "The books."

Mr. Peckleman's eyes bugged out and he sneered. "I already have the books. I want something more! Something to make this game a little more . . . exciting."

Kyle was stumped. He didn't know what else to offer.

A breeze fanned the flames. Made them leap higher.

That's when Marjory Muldauer stepped forward.

"If you win," she said, "you can burn this, too."

She held up her "Go to College Free" card.

53

"Oh, this is interesting," said Mr. Peckleman, rubbing his hands together and leering at the card in Marjory's hand. "Very interesting, indeed."

"Wait," Kyle said to Marjory. "That card's worth thousands of dollars."

"Actually," said Marjory, "it's worth 234,428 dollars. I plan on attending Harvard. For four years."

"Well, that makes your card even more important. You can't just throw it away."

"Yes, I can. Some things are even more important than a free college education. Including 323.443: 'freedom of speech.'"

She handed her card to Mr. Peckleman.

Everyone gasped.

Kyle glanced at the books. He couldn't believe what

he was about to do. He couldn't believe he was even *thinking* about doing it. His brothers would tease him about it for the rest of his life, because it was definitely crazy.

But that didn't stop him.

"Fine," he said, pulling his college scholarship card out of his shirt pocket. "If you win, you can burn mine, too."

Akimi stepped forward. "And mine," she said.

"And mine," said Angus Harper.

"And mine," said twenty-eight other voices as every single one of the Library Olympians stepped forward to hand Mr. Peckleman their orange prize coupons.

"Excellent," giggled Mr. Peckleman, crumbling the thirty-two cards in his hand, wadding them up into one extremely flammable paper ball. "You're on, Mr. Keeley. Mr. Lemoncello won't give you your scholarships. Not without these. Cards must be present to win."

"What's the game?" demanded Kyle.

"Let's see. How about a riddle?"

"Fine. We've got several players who are excellent at solving riddles."

"Who cares? You're the one who made the challenge."

"I know, but . . ."

"What? Afraid you might lose and ruin all of your friends' dreams of a college education at the same time?"

"Riddles aren't my best sport."

"Too bad. I insist on trial by single combat. A duel

between two champions that will decide the fate of everyone and everything else. No one may interfere or offer advice. You, Kyle Keeley, are on your own."

Kyle felt that nervous flutter in his stomach again. Trying to be a hero wasn't always easy or fun.

He looked at his best friend, Akimi.

"Do it."

"You can take him, Kyle," said Andrew.

"Go on, Keeley," said Marjory Muldauer. "Even I'm rooting for you."

Kyle turned to face Mr. Peckleman.

"Okay. I accept your challenge. If I answer your riddle correctly, you don't burn a single book. We take them all back to Mr. Lemoncello's library."

"But if you can't answer my riddle," sneered Peckleman, "if you fail, you and your library-loving friends have to stand here and watch me destroy all of these horrible books and all of these lovely orange cards."

"Deal."

"Oh, this is going to be fun," said Mr. Peckleman. "Let me think. . . . I need a really good riddle . . . one that's almost impossible to solve. . . ."

Kyle waited, giving a little voice deep inside his head time to remind him that *every chance to win is also a chance to lose.*

So Kyle told that little voice to shut up.

Because he needed every brain cell he could spare focused on Mr. Peckleman's riddle.

"All right, Mr. Keeley. Here is your riddle: You are a prisoner in a room with two doors. One leads farther down into the dungeon and certain death; one leads to freedom. There are two guards in the room with you, one at each door. One guard always tells the truth. One always lies. You don't know which is which. What single question can you ask one of the guards that will help you find the door that leads to freedom?"

Oh, man.

Kyle wished somebody else had made the challenge.

But they hadn't. He had.

Concentrate, Kyle told himself. *You can do this thing.*

Okay.

If Kyle wanted to find out which guard told the truth and which one told lies, he could ask, "If I asked the other guard whether you always told the truth, what would he say?" If the guard he asked said, "No," that would mean he was definitely talking to the truth teller. If the guy said, "Yes," that would mean he was the liar, because he never told the truth, about himself *or* the other guard.

Kyle's head was starting to hurt.

"I'm waiting, Mr. Keeley," said Mr. Peckleman, pinching the thin picture book *Earl the Squirrel* between his thumb and forefinger so he could dangle it over the fire pit.

"Gimme a second."

But Kyle had only *one* question to find the right door.

He couldn't do a two-step dance and first find out who

was the truthful guard and then ask him which door to use.

"So . . ."

He had to ask . . .

"My single question," he said, "to either one of the guards . . ."

Everyone was hanging on his every word.

". . . would be . . . 'If I were to ask the other guard, which door would *he* say leads to freedom?' I would then choose the door opposite of the one the guard told me."

"Are you certain, Mr. Keeley?"

"Yes! Because if the guard I ask is the one who always tells the truth, he would tell me the other guard, the lying guy, would point to the door of death. If I asked the guard who always lies, he would also point me to the door of death, because he's a liar. So in either case, I'd choose the door the guard *wasn't* pointing to."

"He's right," declared Marjory. "Right?"

Mr. Peckleman lowered his book.

But not into the fire.

He gently placed it on top of the heap in the little red wagon.

"Well done, Library Olympians. Bravo!"

All of a sudden, Mr. Peckleman had a British accent.

"By being willing to sacrifice everything you thought you came here to win, you have all proven yourselves to be true champions."

Kyle half expected the guy to say "pip pip, cheerio" or something.

Instead, he heard sirens approaching.

The police.

They were flanking a car shaped like a big boot and another one that looked like a pouncing cat.

54

The boot was another playing piece from Mr. Lemoncello's Family Frenzy board game.

So Kyle had a pretty good idea who was driving the bootmobile.

His hero. Luigi L. Lemoncello.

The boot car turned into the motel driveway with Dr. Zinchenko's green-eyed catmobile following close behind.

Kyle couldn't figure out what was going on. Mr. Lemoncello had said he was leaving town. Going to New York or Terabithia, which sounded like it might be in Indiana.

The police cars escorting the two game pieces on wheels had flapping Library Olympics flags attached to their bumpers. They weren't coming to the motel to arrest

Mr. Peckleman. They were just part of Mr. Lemoncello's motorcade.

The boot car skidded to a stop near the patio. Dr. Zinchenko's cat car crawled to a halt behind it. Mr. Lemoncello popped open the boot ankle and stepped out.

"Donald?" cried Mr. Lemoncello, his voice booming across the parking lot. "Extinguish thy flame!"

"I fly with haste to do thy bidding," said Mr. Peckleman, sounding all of a sudden like he was in a play by Shakespeare. He bent down and flipped a switch on the fire pit. The flames disappeared in a poof!

"Gas logs," said Mr. Lemoncello. "Just another part of our glorious charade."

"Huh?" said Kyle.

Mr. Lemoncello was dressed in a bright yellow tracksuit and a half-lemon crash helmet, which he unbuckled and tucked under his arm as he strode onto the patio.

"Please cover those books with their protective tarps," coached Dr. Zinchenko, who was dressed in her standard red leather minidress, scarlet stockings, red high heels, and red-framed librarian glasses.

"Thy wish is my command, milady!" Mr. Peckleman ruffled open a bright blue tarp with a theatrical flourish and draped it over all the squirrel books.

Mr. Lemoncello approached Andrew Peckleman.

"Andrew?"

"Yes, sir?"

"My grandmother isn't Strega Nona, and you don't have a long-lost great-uncle-twice-removed named Woody."

"I don't?"

"No. Meet Sir Donald Thorne, one of the finest actors in all of England!"

Sir Donald, who everybody had thought was Uncle Woodrow "Woody" Peckleman, took off his Blue Jays baseball cap and twirled it in front of his face as he took a bow.

" 'All the world's a stage,' " he said. " 'And all the men and women merely players.' "

"Sir Donald also coached Dr. Zinchenko and me so we might play our own parts with passion and panache." Mr. Lemoncello started imitating himself, acting much more melodramatically than he had in his original performance. "Oh, boo hoo. I, Luigi Libretto Lemoncello, hereby officially declare the games of this first Library Olympiad to be over. Done. Kaput!"

"Wait a second," said Akimi. "That was all an act?"

"Indeed."

"You were very convincing, sir," said Sierra.

"Sir Donald is an excellent coach."

"And thou, sir, art an excellent pupil." Sir Donald took another bow.

"Thank you," said Mr. Lemoncello, taking his own little bow.

256

"But why were you pretending to give up on the library?" asked Kyle.

"To make absolutely, positutely certain that all of you would not do the same. Now, before I made my dramatic exit, I promised I would appoint a new board of trustees for my library on Monday. All public institutions similar to ours have such boards. . . ."

"Indeed they do," added Dr. Zinchenko. "Mostly to raise funds and to make certain the institution fulfills its mission."

"Well," said Mr. Lemoncello, "my library never has to worry about raising funds. Did I mention I'm a bazillionaire?"

"Yes," said Abia Sulayman. "We have heard."

"However, I do need a board of trustees to champion my cause here in Alexandriaville. That's the real reason I hosted these Library Olympics. I told you it was a quest for champions. And it was. I was looking for library lovers willing to stand up and fight for what's right, no matter the cost or personal sacrifice." He paused and looked directly at Marjory. "Even if they did not agree with my way of doing things."

"I'm sorry I took that book," said Marjory.

"We figured somebody would once Mr. Peckleman started passing out his 'Go to College Free' cards. It was a test. To see if you, or anyone else, were here for the wrong reasons. I'm overjoyed that, in the end, you fought so hard to save these books, because believe it or not, Marjory, I, too, love libraries qua libraries. I just don't like saying 'qua.' It makes me sound like a duck."

Everyone, including Marjory, laughed.

"Now then," said Mr. Lemoncello, putting down his crash helmet so he could clasp his hands behind his back and address his Library Olympians, "seeing the results of this final game, I feel confident that I have finally found my first board of trustees. In the end, you all worked together to save the library even though there was no prize except the knowledge, joy, and wonder contained inside the pages of its books."

"But, um, we're not adults," said Akimi.

"Thank goodness. Adults can be so serious and dull. And as you all know, reading and learning are anything but dull!"

"You really want me on your board?" asked Marjory.

"Oh, yes. Couldn't do it without you. Or Andrew."

"I wasn't in the Olympics," said Andrew.

"Minor technicality. You're a trustee now, Mr. Peckleman. Congratulations!"

"But I live in Michigan," said Marjory.

"And my library has state-of-the-art technology, including very high-speed Wi-Fi, so we can all chat via your brand-new smartphones. I need your help—Marjory, Andrew, all of you—to make certain my library is the best that it can be. All I ask is that you always champion freedom of speech, freedom of expression, and freedom of fun!"

"Well, I guess a little fun is okay," said Marjory. "As long as there's always a quiet place for people to read."

"It's why the Electronic Learning Center has soundproof walls." Mr. Lemoncello opened his arms to the group. "So, will you thirty-three new trustees share this quest for truth and knowledge with me?"

"We will!" everyone answered, including Marjory Muldauer, who actually seemed to be enjoying herself.

55

Kyle thought the closing ceremonies were a blast.

Mr. Lemoncello handed out thirty-three full college scholarships before switching off the giant swirling flashlight. A DJ spun dance tunes. There was a huge sheet cake shaped like an open book. On it, written in yellow on a sea of fudgy frosting, were these words: "Open a Book and Open Your Mind."

"Congratulations, Mr. Keeley," said Dr. Zinchenko, who was slicing the cake and passing out pieces. "Oh, I nearly forgot. Mrs. Gause wanted me to give you this. I checked it out of the nine hundreds room."

She handed Kyle a book.

"Mrs. Gause?" said Kyle. "The holographic librarian from when the old library was torn down?"

"That's right. She thought you might like to know why."

Kyle studied the book's cover: *Ohio River Pirates and Scallywags.*

"It's a history book, obviously," said Dr. Zinchenko. "It was written by a teacher at Chumley Prep. I think you'll find chapter eleven to be very enlightening. It's all about a bandit named Ugly Chuck Willoughby, who led the Hole-in-the-Rocks gang, a group of pirates who plundered flatboats along the Ohio River in the late 1700s."

"Wait a second," said Kyle. "Isn't Charles Chiltington's super-rich uncle, Mrs. Chiltington's brother, named Willoughby?"

"Yes. James Willoughby the third. This book will tell you exactly *how* the Willoughby family fortune got its start and why Mrs. Chiltington was so disappointed to find the book on the shelves of the new Lemoncello Library."

"Did she want it banned from the old library, too?"

"Of course. And when Mrs. Gause refused to do her bidding . . ."

"Mrs. Chiltington sent in the bulldozers."

"Actually," said Dr. Zinchenko, "*Mr.* Chiltington is the one in the construction business. Together, they were hoping to rewrite the history that didn't fit their family myth."

"So this book is the real reason why Mrs. Chiltington wanted to take over the Lemoncello Library, isn't it?"

Dr. Zinchenko smiled. "Knowledge can be a very powerful and, for some, frightening thing, Kyle. Especially when it's shared with the whole world, including your neighbors."

"Thank you for this," said Kyle.

He tucked the Ohio history book under his arm and, balancing his cake plate, went over to where Mr. Lemoncello was chatting with Sir Donald Thorne, the actor who didn't look so much like a chicken now that he was out of costume and had taken off his fake rubber nose.

"Oh, you should have seen me when I held that book over the flames, Luigi! I was amazing."

"Yes, Donald," said Mr. Lemoncello politely. "I'm sure you were."

"And when I tricked Mrs. Chiltington into thinking we were co-conspirators? That was some of my best work ever."

"Yes, Donald . . ."

"And my eyes. This is how I bugged them out when I was pretending to be a few sandwiches short of a picnic."

"Very convincing, Donald . . ."

Mr. Lemoncello sounded bored, so Kyle butted in.

"Mr. Lemoncello?"

His eyes brightened. "Excuse me, Donald. Urgent business. I must speak with a member of my new board."

Mr. Lemoncello touched Kyle's shoulder and urged him to step away from Sir Donald Thorne.

Quickly.

"What is it, Kyle?"

"Can I ask you a question?"

"Certainly. In fact, as a trustee of the Lemoncello Library, you are duty bound to come to me with any and all questions you might have."

"Well, sir, was part of this whole Olympic Games thing an attempt to get Andrew Peckleman to like libraries again? Is that why you had Sir Donald pretend to be *his* great-uncle instead of, say, mine or Miguel's?"

Mr. Lemoncello smiled slyly. "Why, Kyle Keeley, do you really think I am that cunning and clever?"

"Yes, sir. That's why your games are so good."

Mr. Lemoncello laughed and nodded toward the far side of the patio, were Andrew Peckleman and Sierra Russell were sharing a piece of cake and laughing.

"My guess is they're talking about their favorite books," said Kyle.

"And my guess," said Mr. Lemoncello, "is that Andrew will be coming to the Lemoncello Library every single Monday, Wednesday, and Friday after school."

"You think so?"

"Certainly. That's when Sierra's there."

Epilogue

On the first day of spring break, two weeks after all the visiting Olympians had gone home, Kyle Keeley biked downtown to the Lemoncello Library.

Charles Chiltington was outside, as usual, walking back and forth on the sidewalk, carrying a protest sign that said "MR. LEMONCELLO'S LIBRARY IS EXECRABLE."

Kyle parked his bike and waved. "Hey, Charles."

"Keeley."

"You want to come inside and check out our reference section? Maybe borrow a thesaurus?"

"What?"

"I totally respect your freedom of expression, Charles. I just think you might be able to express yourself more clearly if you didn't use big words on all your signs. See ya!"

Kyle bounded up the marble steps and entered the

lobby, where the statue of Mr. Lemoncello—with his head tilted back and water spewing out of his puckered fish lips—was gurgling away again. They'd fixed up his slogan about knowledge not shared on the base and added a new one on the side:

A LIBRARY IS AN ARSENAL OF LIBERTY.

In the Rotunda Reading Room, patrons were happily hover-browsing the fiction shelves. Clarence and Clement were checking their email on the built-in desktop tablet computers. Some college kids were huddled around another table, doing some sort of serious research project. And Mrs. Lonni Gause, the holographic librarian, was helping out behind the circulation desk without fear of being bulldozed. Because this library had true champions, intellectual freedom fighters who would do whatever it took to protect it: Mr. Lemoncello, of course, and all the library lovers from the first-ever Library Olympiad, plus Andrew Peckleman.

"Yo, Kyle?" said Miguel as he and Akimi came down one of the spiral staircases. "There's a brand-new game up in the Electronic Learning Center."

"You stand on a platform, slide your feet, and go skating down a frozen canal with Hans Brinker," added Akimi.

"You start out on wooden skates," said Miguel, "but you can win silver ones. Just like in the book."

"It's a brand-new Lemoncello concept," said Akimi.

"Audio-animatronic books. You get to act out a whole novel along with its main characters."

"You also get to skate," added Miguel.

"You guys have fun," said Kyle. "I promised Dr. Z I'd help out in the Children's Room for a couple hours today."

"Cool," said Miguel. "I'm doing that tomorrow. With Sierra and Andrew." He waggled his eyebrows knowingly. "Catch you later, bro."

"Later."

Kyle went into the Children's Room, where kids were reading books with their moms and dads or watching a puppet show or listening to a storyteller or singing along with Mother Goose and her goslings.

"Excuse me," said a small voice behind Kyle.

Kyle turned around. "Can I help you?"

"Is this book any good?"

A tiny boy was holding a copy of *Flora and Ulysses*.

"Oh, it's excellent," said Kyle. "I read it last week. It's all about a squirrel who gets sucked up inside a vacuum cleaner and turns into a poetry-writing superhero."

"Awesome!"

The kid ran to the checkout desk with his prize.

Kyle watched him go and felt great.

Actually, he felt fantastic.

It was definitely another cake day.

THE THIRTEENTH GAME

Are the games really over? Of course not. Here's one final puzzle:

Twenty things you just read,
Twenty things Mr. Lemoncello said,
Were once not allowed to be read
Because of what other people said.

Can you find them all? If so, send an email with your list to author@ChrisGrabenstein.com.

AUTHOR'S NOTE

Writing this book about banned books (which, yikes, might be banned in some places because of its subject matter) made me remember when I was in the fifth grade and bought (with my allowance money) my first subscription to *MAD* magazine. I think it cost less than five dollars for the whole year.

Every month, *MAD* was filled with hysterical satire of TV shows and movies, sarcastic spoofs, and funny fake ads. The thing was pure irreverence in ink and paper.

MAD (along with the *Rocky and Bullwinkle* cartoons) did more to spark

my love of words and humor than anything else during my middle school years.

I remember my monthly installment of *MAD* magazine arrived by mail in a plain brown wrapper because some adults thought its satire and lack of respect for authority made it questionable, maybe even subversive. Many of those adults also thought the magazine should be banned, that impressionable children (like me) should not be allowed to read it.

But read it I did. (Maybe even more hungrily because I knew reading it was considered a form of rebellion.)

My own parents had no problem with my reading *MAD*. I think my father, having seen combat in World War II, had that Greatest Generation's skepticism about blind obedience to rules and those in authority.

When I did improvisational comedy in a Greenwich Village theater—what the *New York Times* described as "basically impudent madness" in a review of our show—we were called the First Amendment Improvisation and Comedy Company. Nightly, we exercised our First Amendment right of freedom of speech to poke fun at politicians and current events and goofy trends and just about anything that needed fun poked at it. We were a living, breathing *MAD* magazine.

And now that I am an author, I always feel a small surge of pride when I read that tiny type printed inside all of my Random House books: "Random House Children's

Books supports the First Amendment and celebrates the right to read."

Doing research for this story, I was amazed at how many children's books have been banned over the years. Not just in the past but as recently as yesterday.

I found myself agreeing with former American Library Association (ALA) president Carol Brey-Casiano, who said, "Not every book is right for every person, but providing a wide range of reading choices is vital for learning, exploration, and imagination. The abilities to read, speak, think, and express ourselves freely are core American values."

I like this bumper sticker of a slogan, too: "Free your mind. Read a banned book."

The ALA sponsors an annual Banned Books Week in September. It's a great time for teachers, students, and librarians to discuss what the First Amendment truly means.

Mr. Lemoncello will definitely be celebrating it this year at his library.

There will be balloons. Cake, too.

And lots and lots of books. Even ones Mr. Lemoncello doesn't really like.

Read more:

ala.org/bbooks/bannedbooksweek
teachhub.com/banned-book-week-activities

MR. LEMONCELLO'S LIBRARY OLYMPICS
BOOK LIST

Here's a complete list of the books mentioned in *Mr. Lemoncello's Library Olympics* that you can find in *your* library. (How many have *you* read?)

☐ *The Adventures of Captain Underpants* by Dav Pilkey
☐ *Anne of Green Gables* by L. M. Montgomery
☐ *The Bad Beginning* by Lemony Snicket
☐ *Because of Winn-Dixie* by Kate DiCamillo
☐ *Birdman of Alcatraz* by Thomas E. Gladdis
☐ *Bleak House* by Charles Dickens
☐ *Blubber* by Judy Blume
☐ *The Book Thief* by Markus Zusak
☐ *The Bravest Squirrel Ever* by Sara Shafer
☐ *Bridge to Terabithia* by Katherine Paterson
☐ *Brown Bear, Brown Bear, What Do You See?*
   by Bill Martin Jr. and Eric Carle

☐ *Bud, Not Buddy* by Christopher Paul Curtis
☐ *The Candymakers* by Wendy Mass
☐ *Charlie and the Chocolate Factory* by Roald Dahl
☐ *Charlotte's Web* by E. B. White
☐ *Criss Cross* by Lynne Rae Perkins
☐ *Earl the Squirrel* by Don Freeman
☐ *Elijah of Buxton* by Christopher Paul Curtis
☐ *Fahrenheit 451* by Ray Bradbury
☐ *Flora and Ulysses: The Illuminated Adventures*
   by Kate DiCamillo
☐ *The Fourteenth Goldfish* by Jennifer L. Holm
☐ *The Girl Who Loved Wild Horses* by Paul Goble
☐ *Goodnight Moon* by Margaret Wise Brown
☐ *Great Expectations* by Charles Dickens
☐ *Green Eggs and Ham* by Dr. Seuss
☐ *Gregor the Overlander* by Suzanne Collins
☐ *Hans Brinker, or The Silver Skates*
   by Mary Mapes Dodge
☐ *Harriet the Spy* by Louise Fitzhugh
☐ *Harry Potter and the Prisoner of Azkaban*
   by J. K. Rowling
☐ *Holes* by Louis Sachar
☐ *The Hunger Games* by Suzanne Collins
☐ *Incident at Hawk's Hill* by Allan W. Eckert
☐ *Inside Out and Back Again* by Thanhha Lai
☐ *It's Not Easy Being Bad* by Cynthia Voigt
☐ *Junie B. Jones series* by Barbara Park
☐ *The Kite Runner* by Khaled Hosseini

☐ *A Light in the Attic* by Shel Silverstein

☐ *Lilly's Purple Plastic Purse* by Kevin Henkes

☐ *The Lion, the Witch, and the Wardrobe* by C. S. Lewis

☐ *Little Women* by Louisa May Alcott

☐ *Lizzie Bright and the Buckminster Boy* by Gary D. Schmidt

☐ *A Long Way from Chicago* by Richard Peck

☐ *The Lorax* by Dr. Seuss

☐ *Lord of the Flies* by William Golding

☐ Maximum Ride series by James Patterson

☐ *Morris the Moose* by B. Wiseman

☐ *Mr. Popper's Penguins* by Richard and Florence Atwater

☐ *Nothing but the Truth: A Documentary Novel* by Avi

☐ *The Odyssey* by Homer

☐ *One Came Home* by Amy Timberlake

☐ *The Paper Airplane Book* by Seymour Simon

☐ Percy Jackson series by Rick Riordan

☐ *Peter Pan* by J. M. Barrie

☐ *Pippi Longstocking* by Astrid Lindgren

☐ *The Postcard* by Tony Abbott

☐ *Sammy Keyes and the Hotel Thief* by Wendelin Van Draanen

☐ *Shabanu: Daughter of the Wind* by Suzanne Fisher Staples

☐ *Sound the Jubilee* by Sandra Forrester

☐ *Splendors and Glooms* by Laura Amy Schlitz

☐ *Strega Nona* by Tomie dePaola
☐ *The Tale of Despereaux* by Kate DiCamillo
☐ *The Tale of Squirrel Nutkin* by Beatrix Potter
☐ *A Tangle of Knots* by Lisa Graff
☐ *Treasure Island* by Robert Louis Stevenson
☐ *Twerp* by Mark Goldblatt
☐ *Ulysses* by James Joyce
☐ *Uncle Tom's Cabin* by Harriet Beecher Stowe
☐ *Ungifted* by Gordon Korman
☐ *The Very Hungry Caterpillar* by Eric Carle
☐ *Walter the Farting Dog*
   by William Kotzwinkle and Glenn Murray
☐ *Watership Down* by Richard Adams
☐ *When Shlemiel Went to Warsaw and Other Stories*
   by Isaac Bashevis Singer
☐ *Where's Waldo?* by Martin Handford
☐ *The Wonderful Wizard of Oz* by L. Frank Baum
☐ *A Wrinkle in Time* by Madeleine L'Engle
☐ *The Year of Billy Miller* by Kevin Henkes
☐ *Yertle the Turtle and Other Stories* by Dr. Seuss

THANK YOU . . .

To the many, many people who helped make this return to Mr. Lemoncello's Library possible.

My wondermous wife, J.J., who reads everything I write before anybody else. If you like my books, it's because she did such a great job editing the first draft. If you don't like them, it's all my fault.

My terrifically creative and supportive Random House editor, Shana Corey. Brainstorming with her is always extremely funderful.

My astounding associate publishing director Michelle Nagler. I love associating with her.

My fantastical designer Nicole de las Heras, who brought the equally fantastical illustrator Gilbert Ford back for another incredible cover.

My amazing literary agent, the dapper Eric Myers,

who has helped me publish nearly forty books over the past ten years.

My team of crackerjack librarians: Amy Alessio, Gail Tobin, Erin Downy Howerton, and Margaret Miles. Without their invaluable assistance, Marjory Muldauer would be all over me for my inexact Dewey decimal numbers. I'd also like to thank librarian Darrell Robertson, whose scavenger hunt game for the first Lemoncello book has been downloaded by nearly a thousand libraries across the country.

My awesometastic "beta readers" in California—the entire Cavalluzzi family: Sunshine, Tony, J.D., Lucy, and Micah. What an amazing family. They even do book-themed dinners and picnics!

My many friends and supporters at Random House Children's Books who have shown Mr. Lemoncello their love: Laura Antonacci, Jennifer Black, Dominique Cimina, Rachel Feld, Lydia Finn, Sonia Nash Gupta, Judith Haut, Alison Kolani, Kim Lauber, Mallory Loehr, Barbara Marcus, Orli Moscowitz, Lisa Nadel, Paula Sadler, Danielle Toth, Adrienne Waintraub, and Ashley Woodfolk. Yes, it takes a village to keep this library open.

The American Museum of Natural History and the New York Public Library for the inspiration of their exhibits "Pterosaurs: Flight in the Age of Dinosaurs" and "The ABC of It: Why Children's Books Matter."

Finally, thank you to all the teachers, parents,

bookstores, and librarians who made *Escape from Mr. Lemoncello's Library* leap to life for young readers through games, extra rebus puzzles, rollicking read-alouds, gala celebrations, bunches of balloons, and incredible scavenger hunts. Thanks for making reading so much fun!